The Apple of Her Eye

By the same author

Araby
Marble Heart
Fire and Ice
Out of the Blue

The Apple of Her Eye

Gretta Mulrooney

ROBERT HALE · LONDON

© Gretta Mulrooney 2009
First published in Great Britain 2009

ISBN 978-0-7090-8775-5

Robert Hale Limited
Clerkenwell House
Clerkenwell Green
London EC1R 0HT

www.halebooks.com

2 4 6 8 10 9 7 5 3 1

Typeset in 11½/16pt Souvenir
by Derek Doyle & Associates, Shaw Heath
Printed in the UK by the MPG Books Group

For Darragh

and
in memory of
David O'Leary

1

I could not cry for my father, could not shed a tear for
months after he died. I wept silent, unseen torrents but
others expect grief to be visible: the moist, bruised eyes,
aching chest and muffled voice of the bereaved. My mourning stayed hidden. His absence was a deep wound that I
bore undisclosed, buried in my heart. Only I knew the love
that had vanished, never to be restored.

I have read that we miss those with whom we have had
uncomplicated, loving relationships less than the people
who have troubled us; something to do with unresolved
matters causing us more woe. Perhaps there is some truth
in that although I think that for myself, I have simply never
fully acknowledged that he has gone. Even now, years later,
I can't quite believe that he won't knock on my door or be
on the end of the phone when I pick it up, saying *tell me
something extraordinary that'll make my toes curl*. I still
miss him, every day. I still feel the chill brutality of his
abrupt exodus, long to hear his voice and feel the comfort
of his embrace.

I had been thinking of him the afternoon I found the

buff-coloured Dauncey Court folder. It was a couple of months after I moved into my flat and I could hear him approving of it, saying that it was *a nice little drum*, the phrase he would utter when we were in the car and passed a particularly handsome home. He used the expression the first time we saw Dauncey, except on that occasion the *little* was used wryly. I was decorating the bedroom and went to look for some old sheets in the oak chest I had kept when we cleared my grandfather's house. The chest had been in storage in my mother's garage, along with the handsome sandalwood gentleman's wardrobe that had been in my room at Dauncey, a chair we called the abbott's chair because my grandfather had bought it at a church fête, and other bits and pieces I'd liked the look of. I recalled having seen some linen at the top of the chest but I hadn't yet had a chance to go through the contents. As I rummaged I came across a folder, tucked below sheets and towels. I opened it and saw that my grandfather had kept some of my sketches from that summer all those years ago, those he would have thought were the best of the scores I produced.

I sat on the floor, cross-legged and fanned them out around me. There was none of my father, even though my mother and Sister Tricia had encouraged me to draw him, no doubt worried about my silences and lack of emotion, suggesting it as a kind of therapy. I couldn't bear to draw him then and I never had in the years since; the thought of it even now was intolerable. If I couldn't have him, real and fizzing with conversation and laughter, I didn't want to create a representation.

The first sketch was the picture of Luca and Cecelia by

the forget-me-not pond, Cecelia holding Daphne in her arms with the silk lead trailing over her elbow. She was wearing a fifties style full-skirted lilac dress that day and I'd found the pleats tricky. Daphne wouldn't stay still for long so the perspective kept shifting. There were drawings of Dauncey Court from different angles and of a reluctant Gina sitting under the arching philadelphus, ankles crossed in front of her and a bowl of apricots and nectarines on her lap; *menopausal old bird with fruit*, she'd called it. One showed my grandfather standing at his easel, paintbrush poised, hanky poking out of his breast pocket. I bent forward and ran my fingers lightly over that dear face. There too was the one of Luca, drawn on an evening when he was serenading Cecelia in the living-room, the sun falling away over the rooftops across the road. He was bending over his lute, his head to one side, his long fingers strumming. That rich voice, vibrating from the deep chest; I recalled it booming through Cecelia's flat, strong and arrogant. Cecelia wasn't in the picture but I could remember exactly where she had been seated, on the small embroidered footstool in front of him, literally at his feet. She was wearing one of the classic linen and silk suits that she favoured and which hung so well on her elegant frame: an A-line skirt and waisted jacket with a brooch on the lapel. Cecelia's favourite song, the one she used to ask for repeatedly, was 'The Wild Mountain Thyme'. She would close her eyes as she listened, fingers linked in her lap, swaying a little. When the refrain came she might join in, her voice wavering: '. . . *will you go, lassie, go and we'll all go together, to pick wild mountain thyme all around the purple heather*. . . .' That evening, though, Luca had been singing Italian songs: *Cari Amici, O Sole Mio, Voce'e Notte, Santa Lucia*, caressing the lyrics with his warm tones;

Chi non demanda
Chi no desia
Santa Lucia, Santa Lucia!

As I had finished sketching Cecelia announced: '*Luca is special, a true artist. One day soon, he will grace the stages of the world.*' He asked to see the picture then but I was reluctant to show it, wanting to take it away and work on his nose, which was finer and straighter than the one I had rendered. As I held it close to me he made the kind of disconcerting move that had always been his forte. He reached out suddenly, pulling me gently towards him by my sleeve and brought his face close to mine. '*Come on, little Marti, no false modesty, let me see!*' His voice was quiet but imperious as always, just as when he would snap his fingers at Cecelia and ask testily if she was ready to go out.

As I blushed he took the drawing from me, scrutinizing it. I looked at his hands, wondering what they would be like against my own skin, feeling little runs of heat along my neck. Then, with a slow turn of his head he looked at me, giving a small, shrewd smile, showing his perfect, even teeth, the ones that Cecelia had paid to have whitened before such treatment was generally available, as common as having a dental check-up. His smile hinted that he knew what I'd been thinking. I looked away, fumbling for my pencils, not wanting his discerning eyes on me.

My fingers found the sketch I had done of Luca and his

friends outside the restaurant in Chelsea Green, the day I
followed him. It was hurried and unfinished but my grandfather must have liked the movement or shading. I had
made an unlikely spy. I laughed, shaking my head, feeling
compassion for that forlorn, befuddled girl who had chased
around the streets with her backpack; *open your eyes,
take care*, I wanted to be able to counsel her belatedly. I
recalled the strawberry milk shakes I had drunk slowly from
my observation post, trying to make them last as long as
possible. Luca was in profile, sunglasses swinging from one
hand, Wilhelm full face, his long hair freed from its pony-
tail that day.

Now suddenly I felt and suppressed the old stomach
tightening Luca used to cause, that awareness of my mouth
drying. I hadn't given Luca Gonzi a conscious thought for
a long while until that afternoon. He and Cecelia were
always there in my memory of course, like a murmuring
stream, Luca in the darker, reedy depths, the tangled places
where you could slip and lose your footing. My fascination
with him had faded with the years but whenever I saw a tall
well-built man of Mediterranean appearance I took a
second look, my pulse skipping. My time at Dauncey Court
was amazing, intriguing, disturbing. I had never stopped re-
imagining it. It turned up frequently in my dreams and
drawings. It was in my blood; it had offered me both salve
and strife. It had distracted me and perhaps distraction is
one of the best soothers of woes. My love affair with the
building itself had inspired my interest in architecture, led
directly to my choice of a career in it.

Night frights, troubled, guilty dreams about Luca had
dogged me for a long time afterwards. Once the police

inquiry was over and he was told there would be no charges I felt both disappointed and relieved. For a while, I wondered if he might seek me out to punish me for being one of his accusers. I waited in a state of listless, delicious fear, glancing around me as I trailed my way to school, biting my nails in apprehension. After long months had gone by I recovered some energy and became absorbed in my drawing classes and exams and the usual teenage pastime of staring in the mirror and wondering what the future holds. If Luca crossed my mind, I imagined that he was living the good life somewhere exotic, or perhaps back in Valetta, the poor emigrant returned wealthy, his social stock high.

I picked up the sketch of Cecelia on her own, the one she had asked me to draw with her holding the Salviati scent bottle. We were in the little diamond-shaped corner library which looked out on to the houses on the opposite side of the square and she saw a woman sitting on her balcony, putting on her make-up. This she found offensive and common. It made her so cross, she pulled too strongly on her pearls and broke the clasp. I learned from her during my sketching that a number of things were *common* or *below the salt*; any eating in the street, wearing brown shoes in town, using tea bags rather than leaves, saying *perfume* rather than *scent* and *serviette* instead of *napkin*. Putting make-up on in public, using a balcony as an extension of your bathroom was a crime in her eyes. *Not the kind of person one would wish to mix with*. I carried on drawing, not sure what I could do with this information but delighted with it; it summed up Cecelia's world, this rich and fascinating place I had wandered into. That was the evening Randolph Smythe interrupted us and upset Cecelia by suggesting she had been a victim of theft, telling her she should go to the police. I could still recall the disdainful look he gave me, assuming that I was one of Luca's 'circus', as he called it.

Finally, I came to a self-portrait. My art teacher had advised me that in order to draw others successfully one first of all needed to understand one's own face; its line and tone, structure, contours and planes, the secrets lying in and beneath the eyes and outward expression. This portrait was one I had drawn in an afternoon in my room, sitting cross-legged on the floor. It was during those days when the police were in and out of Dauncey Court, questioning all of us. After telling Detective-Sergeant Egan about Luca visiting the auctioneers and valuers I had hidden away and undertaken it partly to absorb myself in something, calm myself. My hair was scraped back, giving me a naked, pared-down look. There was a stunned apprehension in my eyes. I looked like a lost girl, or perhaps a girl who could not name what she had lost.

I collected the drawings and sat back, those months crowding into my memory. The decorating no longer seemed a pressing concern. The ring Cecelia had given me was on my right hand; I rarely removed it. I touched the stone lightly. Closing my eyes, I could smell again the pot-pourri aroma of the stairwell at Dauncey Court, the treacle toffee that was always on my grandfather's breath, feel the warm silkiness of Daphne's ears and the tickling softness of the grass that Gina tended so lovingly. I thought of that girl who needed to weep but couldn't, the girl who wore her grief like a carapace. The seductive, ambrosial scent of

Cecelia's rooms came back to me, wafting from the constantly renewed vases of fresh blooms. With it sneaked a reminder of Luca's warm musky skin, the way he used to brush my cheek lightly with the knuckle of his forefinger: *Little Marti, little Marti, how is my woodland sprite today?* I heard an echo of harsh words and tender endearments, felt the strange, violent surge of long-buried emotion.

I wished that I could ring my grandfather and tell him I had found the sketches that I had abandoned in the speed of my departure from Dauncey Court, thank him for having kept them. I assumed he had never mentioned them because he thought I preferred not to have them and all they would remind me of. We would chat about those days, speculate on what might have become of Luca, mull over again what had happened and whether or not he might have been responsible. I could remind him that Randolph Smythe had commented to him one night in the foyer, after a particularly difficult conversation with Cecelia, that if he met old Lucifer himself, Luca would broker a deal. *Oh, he'd buy and sell you before breakfast*, my grandfather had said sagely and Randolph had looked a little startled, adjusting his bow tie.

But my grandfather had died over two years ago, of a heart attack while preparing dinner for an evening with his card-playing cronies. His death meant that the events at Dauncey Court were mine alone now: no one to share them with. I made myself a strong, bitter coffee and paced my newly sanded floors with it, glad of the bracing tang. I knew it would make me jittery but that suited me, suited the restless, scratchy mood that had come over me.

Back I went to the sketches and paced around them, gazing down. Luca looked back at me, direct, insolent, teasing.

In the end, you have to sit and converse with your own ghosts.

2

My grandfather, Liam Breslin, or Bres as he liked to be called, used to visit us every other Sunday, arriving promptly at one o'clock. He was thrilled that we had moved nearer to him at last, on a journey that had taken our family from Bristol via Salisbury to Watford. My father had itchy feet and ambition in equal measures but he promised my mother that the head of upper-school post in a comprehensive just outside the town would be the last move until the twins were ready for secondary education. My mother gave him a certain lowered eyebrows look while tapping her foot and he swore, hand on heart, that he would rather die in a cellar full of rats than have her doubt him. She laughed then and tweaked his nose; she was keen on the increase in income and the en suite bathroom, fitted kitchen and built in wardrobes in her new modern box.

I found Watford unattractive after the handsome towns of the West Country and I loathed the blankness and bleakness of the new house; I missed our tall Victorian terrace with green glass in the fanlights over the front door, the loamy aroma of mildew in the cellar and the fifteen twisty steps to the back garden. However, Watford was nearer London, where I had already decided I wanted to go to university and the truth was I would have moved to Saskatchewan or Murmansk if my adored father had wanted to, so over all my glass was half-full.

Bres would always bring the same gifts with him: a bunch of mixed blue and white flowers for my mother which he presented to her as he kissed her hand, a slab of whisky-flavoured chocolate for my father and a book or sketch pad for me. He made a point of selecting different gifts each for the twins, saying that there was nothing worse than not being treated as an individual. My father, his son, had an affectionately chippy relationship with him and would challenge this remark, leaning against the fridge with a can of beer. He would say something along the lines of: *Really, Dad; so what about torture or starvation or wrongful imprisonment?* My mother juggled a lump of roast meat and controlled simmering vegetables while they bandied phrases, enjoying the cut and thrust. She would sip her glass of dry white wine and blow wisps of hair out of her eyes, pretending annoyance. Eventually, she would shoo them out of the kitchen where they stood, taking up all the space and air while she manoeuvred around them. I liked listening to them, loitering in the doorway. That was when I perfected my natural talent for eavesdropping. It was also when I learned to recognize warm, kindly badinage and differentiate between it and the cutting disparagement that I was to hear later at Dauncey Court.

When Fergus, my father, was killed driving home just six months after starting his new job, my grandfather stepped forward in our lives. Looking back now, I'm amazed that

my mother managed to carry on as she did. I'm not sure
that I would do as well in similar circumstances, a widow
with three children and no career outside the home to
speak of since qualifying as a nurse. When you are a loved
child, you assume that your parents are Olympian gods,
endlessly capable and powerful, as steady and reliable as
the North Star. I was astonished when, three weeks after
my father's death, my mother screamed at me when I
asked for pasta instead of mashed potatoes. Her face twisting, she shouted: *For God's sake, I can't do this, I haven't
had any fucking sleep!* That set the twins off in the background, their three-year-old faces simultaneously crumpling, their wails building to sirenlike volume. My mother
ran to the bathroom, slammed and locked the door. That
bolt shooting into place calmed me and made me understand that I must do something. I took the phone from its
wall mounting and dialled my grandfather's number. *Bres,*
I told him, *my mother is having a nervous breakdown
and the twins are foaming at the mouth.*

He took a cab all the way from Pimlico to Watford. By
the time he arrived my mother had tottered from the bathroom, pink-eyed and raw with tiredness. In silence, we had
eaten charred sausages and cooling lumpy potatoes. The
twins were messing with yogurts when Bres came, wearing
his slippers but otherwise as competent-looking as he must
have been during his brief association with the Irish army
signals corps. He took my mother's hands, pressed them
firmly between his own and told her she looked as weak as
water; *You poor wee creature, take yourself away to your
bed before your legs give out.* Once she had vanished he
informed me that the place looked like the wreck of the

Hesperus. He instructed me to wash up, an activity I was unfamiliar with, and disappeared to bath the twins. I stood on tiptoe and scrubbed at sticky saucepans. I could hear the roar of the hot-water tank filling and my grandfather singing to Ursula and Gregory: . . . *hit the road, Jack, and don't you come back no more, no more, no more, no more. . . .* I blew bubbles from my greasy fingers and pretended that if I squeezed my eyes shut and counted backwards from twenty my father would breeze through the door, briefcase bulging with paperwork, calling that the hunter-gatherer was home, complaining about the traffic and the price of petrol at the bastard garage on the corner.

My father was killed in February, just after I turned thirteen. The driver who slammed into him had reached across the dashboard for a cigarette and in that moment's lapse of concentration had veered straight into him. The police told my mother that he died instantly, would have known nothing about it. She seemed to find some comfort in that but I thought it sounded glib and wondered if it was true or if it was one of those things people in authority said to make the news more bearable, either for themselves or the recipient.

His funeral was on a dark, bitter day, the kind of relentless cold you get in the dregs of winter that makes you feel it will never thaw again. The sky was slumped and steely, without hope. I was so numb, I could recall hardly anything of the crematorium service afterwards. I stood at the front between Bres and my mother. Her eyes were raw and puffy; she had put an icepack on them that morning to try to assuage the burning of her grief. Bres had recommended cold tea leaves but she had snapped at him that she'd look even better with tannin stains all over her face. I was dry-eyed. My eyes had not moistened and they didn't when Jerusalem played or the sounds of sniffing and restrained sobs came from the congregation behind us. I was aware of the odd, murmured phrase: . . . *tragic waste . . . his life before him . . . those poor children.* People got up at the front and spoke: a couple of my father's colleagues, a friend he'd been at college with and others. I didn't hear any of it. I couldn't look at the coffin; I could hardly believe he was in it. None of it had anything to do with me or the vibrant, energetic father I loved. It all seemed like a horrible mistake. I stood next to my mother – the twins had been left with a friend of hers – and I did what I had always done when I felt apprehensive, at the dentist or before a test at school, I recited *Jabberwocky* silently, inside my head. I clung to the comforting, familiar mantra, repeating it over and over. The only words that breached my private recital were when Bres, pale as the white lilies on the coffin before him, took a deep breath and read a final poem, one that my father had loved; Farewell by Anne Brontë.

Farewell to Thee! But not farewell
To all my fondest thoughts of Thee;
Within my heart they still shall dwell
And they shall cheer and comfort me.
Life seems more sweet that Thou didst live
And men more true that Thou wert one;
Nothing is lost that Thou didst give,
Nothing destroyed that Thou hast done.

When he finished, his voice just breaking on the final words, the silence was invaded by people hacking their winter coughs and honking into handkerchiefs. I remembered being at a pantomime with my father one December when many of the audience had colds and him saying, as Jack examined the beanstalk: *Bloody hell, it's like being on a bronchial ward in here.* I slid my fingers in my ears. I was aware of my mother glancing at me through her smarting, heavy-lidded eyes but I didn't care. I shuddered as the coffin slid through the nasty purple curtains and Van Morrison sang *Moondance.* I closed my eyes and pictured mimsy borogoves.

Grief made me mean. I felt callousness thicken my blood, heard it spike my voice, saw it in my hardened gaze. Grief also had a particular tang, I found. No matter how many sweets I ate, and I consumed quantities of chocolate – the milkiest, creamiest I could lay hands on – there was a metallic, bitter taste in my mouth. I wanted to be held, reassured, but whenever my mother tried I brushed her away. When she called me I pretended not to hear. If she asked me to go to the corner shop for tea or bread or other essentials I went reluctantly, slowly, dragging my way there and back so that she was anxious about where I had got to. Then she might say sharply: *Where on earth did you go, the shops at Timbuktu?* Her occasional anger did not truly touch me; I was far away in my own personal Arctic Circle, stranded on an ice floe.

My misery turned my body leaden. Getting out of bed in the morning was a battle, my heavy limbs desiring the warm nest, my eyes needing the curtains to stay drawn.

My room became fuggy and fusty, bathed in a constant half-light, clothes randomly thrown. I was like a little burrowing animal, my supplies of goodies, chocolate, cakes and biscuits beside my bed. The girl who had exasperated her father by hogging the bathroom – *what on earth takes you nearly an hour in there?* – found washing a dreary chore. A cat's lick was managed and a cursory brushing of sugar-caked teeth. Sorrow was grimy and liked to lurk in a cave.

My mother was an only child and her widowed mother lived in Spain, in a retirement village on the Costa del Sol where she had a one-bedroom apartment (so that, my mother muttered darkly, there would be no danger of being visited). To say that they weren't close would be an understatement; my mother would receive postcards now and again referring to people she didn't know and containing news of bridge tournaments, ex-pats' tea dances and golf. Bres's wife Martina, my grandmother whom I was named after, had been dead for twenty years and my father's one sister lived in South Africa so we weren't awash with relatives to help out in a crisis.

After the night of the charred sausages, my grandfather came to see us every weekend for a while, staying over on Saturday night. My mother kept insisting while rubbing her eyes and yawning huge nervous breaths, that she could manage but I looked forward to Saturday afternoons because that was when the valve on the pressure cooker of our lives was released. Bres was the only person I felt any sense of comfort with; he didn't ask how I was feeling or offer sympathy, he just gave me the idea that somehow things had to go on. He would look at me from under his eyebrows and blow a kiss across the room; *Are we winning?* he would say, *have we our boots polished and our rifles cleaned?*

The sound of his finger on the doorbell, *dringdring-a-dringdring*, was a joy. There he would stand, holding a take-away of roast-chicken wraps with salad – the latter being a gesture to my mother's insistence on some greenery with each meal – and sickly-sweet apple turnovers. My mother would take out a cloth splashed with bright red poppies, light a candle and lay place mats. We would pull up our chairs, an illusion of some harmony and balance restored with a man sitting at the table.

Sometimes Bres looked tired and wan. He would wince when one of the twins, usually Ursula, asked yet again where Dad was and when was he coming back? That was the killer question, the enquiry made in a high, innocent voice that cruelly shattered the fiction that we were an ordinary family getting on with life. Then my mother would have to take the twins on her lap and go through the story of Jesus needing Daddy for important work and how he was in Heaven watching over us. I would shovel my food in, trying not to gag at the sickly fable while Bres nodded encouragingly, distracting Ursula as soon as possible from further questions – *but why did Jesus need Daddy?* – *what kind of work, Mummy?* with his trick of taking a coin from his ear.

Once we had eaten, chatting, almost relaxed, my mother went off with a glass of wine to have a long soak and Bres and I entertained the twins, usually with a mixture of TV, stories and games of *find-the-toffee*.

*

For almost ten years I had lived with two abiding truths: that my parents adored each other and me. I nestled in the glow of their devotion, a bookworm, an avid illustrator of my own stories, a studious, orderly only child and the recipient of their undiluted focus. I drew for hours, producing hundreds of sketches which were duly examined, praised and exhibited throughout the house. In other words, I was a more than averagely self-centred pre-pubescent girl. Then, and without my opinion being sought, my carefully structured universe was invaded and colonized. My private name for my brother and sister was The Calamities; the title seemed to encapsulate their darkly harmonized, robotic presences as they staggered around our small house, inflicting repeated random damage and disaster, occasionally ripping my drawings and breaking my pencils and charcoals. When they were asleep they looked cherubic even to my jaded eyes but I hated them for the disruption and chaos they had brought to my life and which was only slightly alleviated by the lock I had angrily fixed to my bedroom door. These strong, conflicting emotions coupled with bereavement were a potent brew; I took to laughing too suddenly and loudly, rubbed my right eyebrow almost bald and bit my fingernails to the quick.

My mother's mourning was evidenced in alopecia; clumps of her thick dark brown hair fell out, exposing small islands of white scalp. Her shock at this was great, as her lush mane had always been a source of great pride to her and she reckoned it to be her most attractive feature. She appeared to be dwindling in front of our eyes; I would find her drifting hairs in the sugar, on the back of the sofa, clogging all the plugholes. The doctor referred her to a trichology clinic where she was told that there was nothing that could be done, that it would probably grow back with time and healing and had she considered grief counselling?

My mother was a part-time Catholic (or, as my grandfather, who had found atheism after a Christian Brothers education declared, a happy-clappy God-botherer.) She occasionally attended small charismatic house groups where believers joined hands and sang along to guitars and tambourines. She had been known to dabble in healing sessions and held a strong belief in guardian angels. My father, a rationalist and sceptic, would furrow his eyebrows at her and comment, *there's one born every minute.*

The grief counsellor, recommended by the parish priest, was a small nun called Sister Tricia who lived in what was called a community house in the centre of town. I would frequently come home from school and find my mother and Sister Tricia ensconced in the kitchen, drinking coffee and eating fig rolls while the twins roamed around their feet, crashing and squabbling. The nun was a tiny woman from a remote North Welsh village, about four feet eleven, dressed in a dark-grey tunic with a lighter-grey cardigan and T-bar shoes. Her feet didn't quite touch the floor so she would tuck them behind the strut of her chair, shifting and creaking constantly to get comfortable. She had allergic rhinitis which gave her permanently pinkish nostrils and a frequent and irritating sniff reflex. My mother, a tall rangy figure, loomed over her and enjoyed patronizing her, even occasionally stroking her arm as if she was a little pet. She did have hamster-like qualities, with her sensitized, twitching nose and quick movements. I think that Sister Tricia was frightened of the twins who were large, robust children and she covered this terror with a simpering, slushy tone towards them. I disliked her invasion of our space, her pebbly dishwater eyes, her sniffing and the way she swallowed before she spoke. She lowered her voice and clasped her child-sized hands together whenever she was about to say something significant, usually some sugary psychobabble platitude that my mother would drink in and use on me: *Marti, I'm sensing resentment from you....are you sure that's really what you're trying to say to me . . . it's all right, this pain and anger is a part of your grief journey.*

The nun brought books that my mother became absorbed in, self-help tomes: *Finding The Path, The Journey Within, Talking To Angels.* Through Sister Tricia my mother was embracing the view that my father's death was part of a mysterious, bigger plan and had a meaning that we might never know or understand. With the diminutive nun's encouragement, she had written a note to the killer driver, telling him she forgave him. I hated him and wanted revenge, preferably life imprisonment. For me, Sister Tricia provided little laminated cards printed with daisies, rainbows and sunny blue skies. On the backs of these were saccharine banalities that made me grind my teeth: *choose the sunlight, not the shadows; catch the star that holds your destiny; embrace the day and joy will find you.* They were impossible to tear in their resistant plastic so I cut them into tiny pieces with scissors and left them lying on the kitchen table. The destruction didn't make me feel any better, but sourly affirmed my hostility.

Lying in bed at night, I wondered if the driver had a daughter and if she knew that he had murdered someone. When my mother reminded me that Jesus had said to turn the other cheek, I said that I preferred the idea of an *eye* for an *eye*.

Sister Tricia gave me wary glances as I silently moved around the worktops with a deliberate tread, making myself slabs of toast and peanut butter and brewing the herbal tea which I didn't much care for but had been my father's favourite. When I tasted that gingery flavour I could savour the memory of his light kisses on my cheek. Sister Tricia would ask me brightly about my day, how was school, did I have any homework, what was my favourite subject? Mouth full, I would mutter, looking away.

One evening, when my mother was busy upstairs bathing the twins in a scene that always resembled a battle-field recently vacated by Attila the Hun, Sister Tricia glided up to me, laid a small hand on my shoulder and looked at me meaningfully.

'Your mum needs a lot of support just now, you know. I understand that you have your own grief but you have to be her friend as well as her daughter. You could maybe help a bit more with your brother and sister?'

I had been standing gazing out of the living-room window, watching the brilliant crescent moon, lost in my own hazy thoughts. Frequently, I would find myself drifting in a paralysed, deadened bemusement, as if I was standing apart from the world, glimpsing it through a veil, hearing through a muffled barrier, my ears seemingly packed with cotton wool. The hand on my shoulder was a shock even though it was as light as a moth's wings. Stunned, I could-n't open my mouth, which unfortunately encouraged Sister Tricia to say more.

'Do you think, Martina, that you are perhaps being just

a little bit self-absorbed? This is a family, there are four people hurting here. And you know, your daddy wouldn't want you to let yourself go. Your hair is looking so lank, it could do with a good wash, and your neck and nails. Mummy doesn't like to say anything but, well, girls at your age need to be careful about personal hygiene.'

I peeled my eyes away from the hanging moon, looked at her and walked away, humming.

Dedicated to her helping task, within months Sister Tricia had encouraged my mother to network with other widows whom she visited; she maintained, hands pressed close, that *a trouble shared was a trouble halved.* I saw her as a small, busy spider, drawing needy victims into her web. This silken weave of widows meant that on some evenings our living-room was full of wan women, Paulines, Bridgets, Annies and Ruths with brave faces and exhausted eyes, drinking wine or coffee and planning sisterly walks and trips to theatres and cinemas. Sister Tricia bobbed around them, sipping apple juice, complimenting them on hair dos and clothes, congratulating them in her special syrupy voice for their bravery: *You saw the bank manager on your own? Well done, you!* The widows wore too much lipstick and emitted a desperation that made the air hard to breathe. After enduring their well-meaning questions I skulked upstairs, hearing their voices grow louder as bottles emptied. My home had been invaded and the nun was the cause of this frantic occupation.

'Sister T is only trying to help, you know,' my mother said one evening in the brief, blissful calm that descended between the twins going to sleep and the influx of bereaved women. 'I think you should try being more welcoming.' Self-conscious about her hair loss, she had taken to wearing a scarf around her head all the time, tied in a bow at the nape of her neck. It made her look oddly demure and nunlike and it seemed to me just another sign of Sister Tricia's influence on our lives.

'I don't like her,' I said.

'You can be polite even if you don't like someone. Anyway, what's there not to like?'

'She talks rubbish and she's patronizing. She doesn't know anything about us, really, but she acts as if she's one of the family.'

'That's not fair, Marti. She's widely read on the subject of bereavement and she's been on counselling courses. She means well and she puts herself out in ways she doesn't have to.'

'She implied that I'm smelly.'

'Ah. Maybe she's not always as sensitive as she could be.' My mother smiled encouragingly. 'But, as you mention it, a long shower wouldn't go amiss, and the appropriate use of products.'

Cornered, I came up with my trump card. 'Dad wouldn't have liked her either.'

'You don't know that.' My mother stopped folding sheets, her fingertips straying unconsciously underneath the scarf to one of her bald patches.

'Yes I do, I do know it. He hated mumbo jumbo and triteness, he'd have laughed at those clichéd cards she brought me.'

My mother sighed. 'I don't know what's got into you. Believe me, your father of all people would have understood that I need this help just now and he wouldn't approve of your attitude. I managed to throw the cards you cut up away before she saw them. It's hurtful to do that to someone's gift. Marti, you know that. Why do it?'

I threw down the book on landscape drawing that I'd been reading. 'My dad was killed by a stupid man for the sake of a stupid fag,' I said, kicking a Calamity's tricycle out of the way as I stomped to my room.

Bres was caretaker of Dauncey Court, a block of stately Edwardian mansion flats in Pimlico, built around two sides of one of those private garden oases that grace London. He had come to this job in later life after a varied career including running a bakery in Derry, the city where he was born, two years in the Irish army, time-share sales, cab driver, bookseller, carpenter, London tour guide and pub manager. During his sixtieth year he had landed the caretaking job, which came with a basement flat, one of its big attractions with its large rooms and high ceilings. We had visited him there once and I loved the place the moment I saw it; its elegant proportions and simple lines appealed in a way I didn't understand except that for the first time I realized that a building could be *beautiful*, could make the heart sing. I had particularly enjoyed travelling up and down from the basement to the sixth floor in the claustrophobic lift, one of those old-fashioned dark wooden ones with metal fold-back doors at each floor. I liked frightening myself with its squeaking ascent and descent, imagining what would happen if it plummeted and I had to climb the ropes to safety, as I had seen done in several films.

Bres would regale us with stories about the people who

lived in Dauncey Court, although he never mentioned full names, saying as he tapped the side of his nose that he had to be careful about confidentiality; the managing agents were very hot on privacy. So we heard mysterious tales of Mr C, the company director who had a gambling habit and a different boyfriend every week, Mrs W, an artist who kept a pet ferret against the conditions of her lease, Mr and Mrs P who accused all their maids of stealing, Mrs B who was under the sway of a Maltese gigolo and Miss L who had been a film actress in the fifties and was drunk by nine every morning. *More money than sense*, Bres would say as he described them, shaking his head, *and especially the rich old ladies*.

He was responsible for the security and maintenance of the building, making sure that the boilers and heating system functioned, the lifts operated, the public hallways were kept clean and that no riff-raff penetrated the dry, rarefied atmosphere of the mansion. Every morning, he buffed up the brass plate declaring the name of the building and checked that the buzzer for each flat was working. He also catered for the particular needs of what he called *old money*; he knew who to contact if a chandelier, a Hogarth print, a Queen Anne table or priceless rug brought back from Abyssinia in the 1920s needed repair or cleaning. I had never been inside one of the flats but had listened, enthralled, as he described them; each one the size of four detached houses, with drawing-rooms, dining-rooms, libraries, bathrooms, kichens, utility rooms and, of course, spare rooms for live-in help. Our small modern house, he said, would tuck into a corner of one of the flats, like a baby kangaroo in its mother's pouch, an image which fascinated me.

It was music to my ears, therefore, when Bres took me aside one Saturday evening in June while the twins were trying to strangle each other amongst a jumble of toys, crushed books and crumbled biscuits and asked if I'd like to come and stay with him for the summer holidays. It would be better, he suggested lightly, than kicking my heels around Watford. I had already been dreading the long days, anticipating undiluted exposure to The Calamities, Sister Tricia, the widows, my mother's long-suffering glances and references to angels and *the bigger picture*. I felt like a drowning girl who had been thrown a lifebelt. I nodded frantically at Bres, checking through a dry throat that my mother agreed. Oh yes, he told me, it was all sorted, if I was keen; he'd cleared it with the management at Dauncey Court too. A change of scene could be a bit of a boost to the old system. And, he added, he could do with the help and company, he wasn't getting any younger – maybe I could do the odd scrambled eggs and run some messages. I knew that last comment was thrown in to make me feel better and I pursed my lips wisely, gripping my fists with joy. Oh and, he said vaguely, rustling the evening paper, a bit of a wash and brush up would be an idea. My mother came in from the kitchen then carrying a plate of garlic bread and when Bres told her that the summer plan was fine with me she looked sad but relieved and offered me the crustiest slices of bread, my favourite.

That night I turned on the shower and stayed under it for ten minutes, scrubbing my skin. Then I ran a bath, liberally pouring scented salts in. I lay there in the silky water, a tiny ripple of selfish cheer in my heart for the first time since that evening in February when the solemn-faced police came to the door, asking gently for my mother. I thought about Bres's roomy flat, my own luxurious space, the streets of London – museums and parks – on my doorstep and the hushed, private gardens of Dauncey Court where I could sprawl and read and draw to my heart's content without interruption, questions, mayhem and the unwanted ministrations of Sister Tricia. *O frabjous day! Callooh! Callay!* I whispered.

I topped up the hot water and dunked my head, performing my baptism into a different life.

3

I loved my father more than my mother when I was young; I didn't understand this until he died, I hadn't needed to. We were alike physically and in our tastes, dispositions and temperaments. We laughed at the same things, saw and experienced the world in the same way. We even had the same way of eating, methodically and neatly, cutting food into equal sections and ensuring a portion of each ingredient on the fork. People, including my mother, said I was the spitting image of him and when he had gone I resented her with a fierce bitterness. I didn't actually form the thought, *why couldn't it have been her*, but I certainly felt that emotion and it came out as surly disengagement. My mother must have sensed this and it is to her credit that she never mentioned it or held it against me, even though I must have tried her patience beyond endurance. I did almost nothing to help her during those months after my father's death, yet she tolerated my unpleasantness and gruffness. She kept out of my way when I was packing to go to Bres's, taking the twins for a walk in the park. When she dropped me at the station she gave me a small silver locket with a tiny photo of my father inside. I recognized it as a picture from our holiday the year before in France. I didn't want it, the immediacy of it, but I grunted some kind of thanks and ran from the car, hot salt searing my throat.

Bres greeted me at Euston station with his usual salutation to me: *what's the news, o my bold shelmalier?* My father had explained to me many years before that *shelmalier* was a corruption of the French *chevalier* and had probably been introduced to Ireland via the long association between the French and the Irish Republican cause.

'The news is that I'm fit and ready for the summer,' I told him.

'Well, and aren't you looking like yourself, and very smart, too,' he replied in his deep, fruity voice that reminded me of the tea and whiskey loaf he made. 'Shall we promenade?'

He took my bag while I adjusted the straps of my rucksack, then held his arm out and I slipped mine into the crook. He was wearing pressed navy trousers with sharp creases and a white short-sleeved shirt; his caretaker uniform; they suited his slim, compact figure. On his head was a trilby. Bres always wore a trilby hat outdoors, all year round; he maintained that it kept him warm in winter, cool in summer. His winter one was dark grey, his summer one light blue. He bought them from a specialist gentlemen's outfitters near Sloane Square. My father used to say that the hat made him look like a benign gangster. He stepped lightly, throwing his left leg slightly as he walked and now and again I had to skip to match his pace as we made our way down to the Underground. Victoria was bustling with tourists when we stepped from the escalator and weaved our way out, crossing the roads and heading into Ebury Street. Bres pointed out the blue plaque to Ian Fleming and the flat where, he informed me, the author of James Bond had invited many ladies whom he romanced in the manner of his hero.

I raised an eyebrow at him. 'Do you mean,' I asked, 'that he loved them and left them?'

'That's about it. He was a bit of a cad, I believe. There's a fella of the type at Dauncey Court, you'll meet him soon enough. Thinks he's God's gift to women.'

'The one you call the strumming gigolo?'

'That's right. Did I ever advise you that you can tell a gentleman by the shine on his leather shoes?'

'Yes, you've told me that.' I looked down at Bres's brilliant, sturdy black lace-ups.

'Well, the gigolo wears sandals and sneakers or trainers, or whatever they're called – that tells you all you need to know. Will we have fish and chips for lunch? The pub on the corner does a take-away.'

We bought our fish and chips, plaice for me and cod for Bres at the pub, the Fife and Drum, which had a notice written on a blackboard just inside the door: *I'd rather have a bottle in front of me than a frontal lobotomy.* There were a number of young business types in there, talking quickly and intently. The man who served us was in his early twenties, Australian and good-looking in a long-haired, blond surfer style. He smiled at me, an easy, open grin as Bres introduced me and I looked away, embarrassed because he was so handsome. I was at the stage of early adolescence where I was becoming aware of attractive men but squirmed if my glances were noticed. There was another, sterner sign over the door facing us; *Please leave quietly, this is a residential neighbourhood.*

We carried our lunches in their plain brown boxes for the few minutes to Dauncey Court. Although I had seen it before, the place still took my breath away. It made all the buildings in my home town seem squat and ugly, especially the drab look-alike dwellings on the estate where my family lived. It sat, majestic and solid in the noon sun, its red bricks glowing a deep, burnished chestnut. The great square sash-windows caught and reflected the light, the glass gleaming, the white gloss paintwork immaculate. Climbing roses, deep pink and pale apricot, intertwined with clematis around the high bronze railings that hid the lush gardens from the public gaze. We passed the ornate archway and steps leading to the double oak doors with inset panels and gleaming brass handles and went to the side of the building and the entrance to the basement, a plain metal door.

Bres's flat was down one flight of stairs; at the far end of his corridor was the boiler room and the back exit to the bin area. He fetched vinegar and ketchup from the kitchen and we sat on sofas in his living-room, eating from the boxes and watching the horse racing from Newbury. My mother would never have allowed this kind of behaviour; she insisted that all meals had to be taken at the table. She'd read lots of articles about family life being eroded by TV suppers, food eaten on the hoof. While she focused on such small matters, a far bigger attrition, my father's death, unexpectedly took place.

I looked around while Bres followed the race. The living-room was large and square with plain cream walls, varnished floorboards and a rug, pale blue with yellow flowers. It was pleasingly uncluttered, minimalist even, with a wonderful absence of toys, crushed foodstuffs and greasy pawmarks. My armchair matched the brown leather sofa Bres was sitting on, a deep thirties style with brass studs around the arm edges. The leather was worn, creased into a warm comfort by previous owners. There was an oak dining table by the window, the kind with leaves that pull out, and several bookcases. On the walls were paintings executed by Bres in his own inimitable style which he called a cross between Matisse and Warhol, realism blended with blurry brush-strokes. They were all scenes of Derry, which he had left over thirty-five years ago but never tired of reproducing from old photographs: the great fire at the Guildhall, the bakery where he once worked, the view from the city cemetery to Donegal, a busy Saturday in steep Shipquay street, the Victorian splendour of Magee College. I had never been to the city but felt a kinship with it because I had known these oil paintings all my life. James Joyce, Bres informed me, had spent his days as an exile from Ireland and recreating it and it was the same for him with the city of his birth. I didn't know whether Bres's paintings were any good but I liked their boldness and strong colours. It was accepted in the family that I inherited my talent for drawing from him, that he was the artistic source.

'Come on, Sky Rocket!' Bres yelled at the screen, urging a horse on with a pointed chip. When it came in first he whooped and popped a crispy wedge of batter in his mouth. 'That's two hundred in the coffers,' he told me. 'A great horse, Sky Rocket, nearly as good as one I once had shares in.'

'Is there anything you haven't done, Bres?' I asked,

thinking of all the jobs and interests I'd heard him mention over the years.

He looked at me, frowning with thought. 'To my great regret, I never danced with Margot Fonteyn,' he said.

When we'd finished eating, he showed me to my room, which was past his and the bathroom and, like the living-room, looked up into the deep green garden. It was twice the size of my room at home and held a high single bed, a sandalwood wardrobe and a chest of drawers as well as a slim desk. On the chest of drawers was a large clock with a brass surround and Roman numerals.

'Will it do?' he asked. 'The walls are bare but I thought you could put your drawings on them.'

'It's lovely,' I said, listening to the peace and quiet, the muted chords of someone practising a piano, the muffled *snip snip* of shears being wielded by the gardener.

'Madam will stay then?' Bres executed an elaborate bow, winking.

'Madam will.'

That night and for many nights to come I slept until morning, without waking frequently in a heated panic and longing for my father. I still dreamed of him, wanted to dream of him and summoned his image each night as I closed my eyes. My bed was solid and encompassing, holding me in a close embrace. The regular *tick tock* of the clock reassured me, like a steadily beating heart. The garden outside my window was hushed, the air fragrant with honeysuckle, climbing roses and those secret flower scents that only enhance the dark and vanish with the daybreak. None of the mayhem of London penetrated the quiet seclusion of

Dauncey Court; it was as if the residents paid for tranquillity as well as window cleaning and heating.

There were just a couple of rules, Bres had explained. I mustn't talk about anybody who lived in Dauncey Court outside the building; the tenants forked out big bucks for their privacy. I mustn't call on anyone unless I had been invited and I must be very careful with the key I had been given to the garden and keep it in a safe place. I solved this problem by buying a metal clip and attaching it to the waistband of my jeans.

The building contained twelve flats, two on each of the floors, the front doors facing each other across a wide landing, on either side of the lift. On my second day at Dauncey Court, Bres introduced me to Elena, the cleaner who came every morning to vacuum the landings and stairs, mop the black-and-white diamond-shaped tiles in the foyer and polish the mahogany banisters. She was a small rotund woman in her fifties with black hair pinned in a high bun and a gap between her front teeth which she told me was considered lucky in Argentina, where she came from. She wore velour tracksuits to work and a pungent vanilla scent which drifted down the stairwell as she pushed her upright Hoover around. Bres had informed me that she was thorough and her beady eyes missed nothing. He'd added that he wouldn't want her to get him in a headlock and I wondered if she was one of the women whom my grandfather often appeared to be fending off. I had heard my mother comment that because he was nice-looking, fit for his age with a full head of hair, he would inevitably attract the ladies. My father used to joke about this, asking him if he was walking out with anyone. Bres always replied that his wife had been the only woman for him, there was no one who could hold a candle to her and any others were whistling in the breeze.

'You come to help your granddad?' Elena asked me, hitching up her purple elasticated trousers. She had wide gold rings on both hands and chipped red nail varnish.

'In a way,' I said.

'That's good. The young people in this country, they don't care about the old ones much.'

'Bres is only sixty-two,' I told her, even though to me he seemed ancient. 'He wouldn't like to be referred to as old, he says he always feels eighteen.'

'You've got a tongue in your head,' Elena said, but not nastily, flicking her duster along the banister.

We moved aside as a young man ran up the stairs two at a time carrying a deep box of flowers. I could see bright red amaryllis, pink carnations, creamy roses and aspidistra leaves. Their perfume washed over us as he smiled hallo and carried on.

'Mrs Buchanan's flowers,' Elena said, sniffing the air. 'Every morning that chap comes with them, half nine on the dot. I tell him he could take the lift but he says he prefers the stairs, keeps him fit. When I win the lottery I'll have fresh flowers every day and I'll never use stairs again.'

Bres also took me around to introduce me to any available residents so that if they noticed me about the place 'it wouldn't frighten the horses'. Some of them were away for the summer; they had holiday homes in Italy, Spain and France. The only ones in that morning were Miss Leycroft, the faded actress, Mr Courteney, the gambler, and Mrs Buchanan, the woman of strumming gigolo fame. Sylvie

Leycroft lived on the top floor and was standing on the landing, looking vague and the worse for wear as we opened the lift door. She was shoeless and there was a huge hole in her tights, allowing her right big toe to escape. I had the impression that she might have been loitering there for some time, as if she had forgotten what she'd come out for. Her navy-blue dress was askew, with the bodice buttons misaligned and what looked like gravy stains on the skirt. Her eye make-up was smudged, giving her a bruised appearance. She nodded at me dreamily when Bres explained who I was, hiccuped and asked him if he'd like a whisky. When he said it was a little early she gave him a bleary smile and darted back into her flat. Bres gave me an old-fashioned look and made glass-raising movements with his right hand. I nodded wisely, feeling suddenly grown up and worldly.

'At some point,' Bres said quietly, 'she'll try to give you money and ask you to run to the shop for a couple of bottles. Refuse, politely but firmly. Got that?'

I nodded. Miss Leycroft had left traces of stale scent and whisky on the air, the smell of exhaustion. On the way down the stairs we met Mr Courteney coming up, a slim, tall, grey-haired man with a healthy tan, wearing a green linen suit. He inclined his head graciously towards me and gave me the sweetest of smiles, saying he hoped I had a jolly fun time in London. 'A lovely fella but going to the dogs, he owes at least a thousand on maintenance charges,' Bres told me as soon as we were downstairs.

As he rang the bell of number three on the second floor, Bres whispered, 'This is where the gigolo resides,' and I felt a thrill tickle my stomach. I had no idea what a gigolo might

look like; I imagined a man with hooded eyes, a thin mous-
tache and drenched in aftershave. Luca wasn't there that
day, though; it was Cecelia who answered the door after a
long pause, during which she examined us through the
spyhole in the centre panel. Eventually she opened the
door just an inch or two, gazed myopically through, then
pulled it wider. I looked at her bright hazel eyes, fine bones
and neat mouth and even though she seemed very old, I
knew she must once have been beautiful.

'Ye-e-e-s?' she said, in a low drawl.

'Good morning, Mrs Buchanan. I just wanted to introduce my granddaughter, Martina. She's staying for a while
with me.'

'How do you do, Martina?' Cecelia said, slowly and
precisely, transferring her walking cane from her right hand
to her left and holding her hand out to me. I'd never heard
anyone speak in that kind of accent in real life, it was like
listening to an actress in an old black-and-white film, someone who would be in a drawing-room with servants, someone who would ring a bell for afternoon tea.

'I'm very well, thank you,' I told her.

Her hand was dry and chilly, the skin like the paper
between the photographs in albums. She gave me a little
smile and a nod, lightly touching the buttons on the front
of her tailored jacket. She was graceful and thin, like a
mannequin in a shop window, but one with wrinkles. Her
pale-blue eye shadow, face powder and coral lipstick had
been applied deftly and she wore a coffee-coloured fine
wool suit with a cream silk shirt, earrings and pearls. Her
shoes were cream leather, with a small heel and one coffee-
coloured diagonal stripe across the toes. Her hair was thin

too, dyed a dark brunette and coiled in a French pleat with a jewelled clasp holding it in place; later, as my education in the finer things of life progressed, I was to discover that it was made of white gold and diamonds. She had a fresh, deep apricot-coloured rose pinned to her jacket lapel. She looked like someone who was about to go out to a garden party or celebration but Cecelia dressed like this every day, even if she only ventured out to her hairdresser or for coffee.

'You speak clearly, how lovely,' she said to me. 'So many young people mutter and it is difficult to understand them.'

I was nonplussed but I smiled, nodding. There was a light miaow and a delicate Siamese cat the colour of bitter chocolate snaked suddenly around Cecelia's feet, nudging her ankles. As the door pushed wider I saw a small, slim woman in a white apron arranging flowers in a crystal vase, smoothing the aspidistra leaves between nimble fingers.

'Now, Daphne,' Cecelia said, looking down, her voice softening, almost like a purr, 'you are a bothersome pussums. I'll see to your snack in a moment. Is the electrician coming today?' she asked Bres, suddenly brisk again. 'Luca really does need his shower fixed, it's most inconvenient for him at present.'

'He's due at eleven, Mrs Buchanan. Will you be in, or would you like me to sort it out?' My grandfather was speaking differently, more smoothly, his tone lower. I listened with interest, realizing that Cecelia must top the pecking order in Dauncey Court.

Cecelia pursed her lips. 'I shall be out, I am going to my dressmaker. So kind of you, if you could see to it. Fortunata is too timid to deal with any difficulties and her English deserts her. One can't trust tradesmen not to make a mess or break something and Luca is rehearsing today, you know; a concert which will be on the radio.'

'Very nice,' Bres commented. 'Just leave it to me, I'll make sure everything is shipshape.'

'Thank you. Goodbye,' she said abruptly, checking that Daphne had gone back inside and closing the door swiftly.

'Is Mrs Buchanan very rich?' I asked Bres later as we waited for the electrician and ate chocolate biscuits.

'Rich as Croesus and daft as a brush. It amazes me that she takes such care looking through her spyhole but she's got a crook living under her roof. You can get a butcher's at her flat when the shower is being done; a very elegant set up. But for all her wealth and goods and haughty style she's a lonely old woman, or was until she met Mr Luca Gonzi. That's how come the gigolo has her wrapped round his little finger.' Bres wound a sliver of gold biscuit-wrapping around his little finger in illustration, pulling it so tightly that it snapped.

Cecelia had bought the flat in Dauncey Court after her husband died, when she was seventy; they were retired and living in Nice at that time and she decided to move back to London, where she was born. Her husband, Bartholomew Buchanan, had been a diplomat and Cecelia had travelled the world with him for forty or more years. Bartholomew was from an old Scottish family who had been rewarded with land on Loch Lomond by Malcolm II for helping him fight off Nordic invaders. Cecelia's people were Gray-Nortons, rich landowners in Suffolk. She and Bartholomew had no children and Cecelia had only one living relative, an elderly cousin, Randolph Smythe who lived in St John's Wood.

On that morning when the electrician was working in Luca's room, I wandered around the flat while Bres was monitoring the work and making the 'sparks', as he called him, a cup of tea 'to keep him sweet'. Bres had advised me that I could look in any room with an open door. The hall-way ran the length of the flat and was twice the width of our house. There was one huge sash window at the far end from the door, through which the sun flooded, gleaming on the frames of the paintings lining the walls; Constables, an Orpen, two Degas, several Van Goghs and a number of gloomy hunting scenes with dogs and horses. The carpet was rose-coloured and deep; my flip-flops sank into the pile. There were chairs and occasional tables placed at intervals, with china figurines, pot-pourri and vases of flow-ers, the freshly delivered ones and pink and lime oriental lilies, so that the still air was drowsy with perfume. Halfway down the hallway on the left were two open doors; the first led into a vast dining-room decorated in deep reds and cream with a great square mahogany table and red velvet chairs, glass fronted cupboards full of china and glasses, a chandelier and more paintings. Through the second door was a drawing-room painted in pale blues and whites, with two large sofas and several smaller armchairs, an old-fash-ioned radiogram and a harpsichord. Two chairs were posi-tioned by the windows, facing each other, and beside each chair was a tapestry stretched on a frame. They were both being worked on, needles had been left threaded at the edges of the frames; one was a circle of lilies, in creams, pale yellows and greens, the other an oblong, abstract pattern in terracotta, gold and dark orange, the colour of Seville marmalade.

On the deep window ledge was a large black and white photograph in a silver frame, of a young man and woman. I knelt and looked, careful not to touch; Bres had warned me not to go too near anything. I knew from the fine cheekbones that the woman was Cecelia and guessed that the man must be her husband. They were sitting on the deck of a yacht in a harbour with palm trees in the background, holding cocktail glasses up to the camera. The man was handsome and well-built, with a confident gaze as he lounged in his chair, shirtsleeves rolled up, legs crossed. Cecelia leaned in towards him, one hand on his arm, slim and elegant in a skirt, blouse and open-toed high-heeled shoes. Her hair was shoulder-length, held back with a flowing scarf. She was smiling, happy, animated.

I moved through the rooms on the other side of the hall: a light, L-shaped kitchen full of slim, gleaming stainless steel appliances, a laundry room, a walk-in cupboard full of coats and shoes and a storeroom with deep shelves crammed with cleaning materials on one side and jars, bottles and cans of food on the other. The culinary section contained boxes marked Fortnum & Mason, three wide wine racks and tins of tea and coffee with the elegant script of Harrods on the sides. Fat bottles of champagne were ranked along the floor. I stared; I had never seen so much food before. It made our cupboards at home seem bare. I read labels, puzzled; what, I wondered, were Morning Glory in brine and Osso Bucco in wine and pepper sauce? I was a thin teenager with a huge appetite; my mouth watered.

I moved on, thinking of that food, past several rooms

with closed doors and four in a row with the doors propped ajar. Three of these were in a chaotic state, with dustsheets covering the floors; a bathroom was stacked with cans of paint and rolls of wallpaper, while the middle two had been knocked through into one, with bare brickwork showing on the walls. The fourth, a bedroom, held a king size bed, a tall wardrobe and one large painting of a storm at sea. Several stringed instruments of varying shapes and sizes were lined up against one wall and there was a music stand with a book open. On a shelf by the bed was a diamond-patterned decanter with an amber liquid. The electrician was sipping tea in the bathroom and examining an array of tubes and bottles on a shelf over the sink. He nodded at me, grinning and held out a heavy, brown-black bottle.

'Have a sniff of this.'

I took it and breathed in a complex, delicate scent, resinous and invigorating. The tiny gold label informed me that it was skin salve with bergamot, golden amber and olive wood. 'It's lovely,' I said.

'Should be,' the electrician told me, pouring out a small quantity which he rubbed on his nose. 'You wouldn't get much change from a hundred quid for it. The chap who lives here likes himself.'

'You'll be in trouble if you get caught,' I warned.

He winked at me. 'I won't, though. You have to live a bit dangerously, don't you?'

Back in the dining-room, I longed to draw out one of the deep, high-backed chairs and sit on its velvet seat below the striking chandelier. I had never been amongst such exquisite things, surrounded by such easy opulence and refinement. I didn't know the names of many of the antiques, that the china was Dresden, the painting in Luca's bedroom an original Turner and the one of a sad girl over the fireplace in the sitting-room a Modigliani, that the cabinet in the hallway was Louis XIV. I only knew that these things were beautiful and pleasing. Later, when Cecelia saw some of my drawings and decided I had an artistic eye, she took me around the flat, carefully explaining the provenance of her works of art, her furnishings and figurines and precious scent-bottle collection. I was present too when the solicitor's assistant came to take the inventory that Randolph insisted on after the seventeenth-century Chinese snuff case went missing from the sitting-room. I listened in growing amazement at the insurance value of Cecelia's possessions. On that first morning in her dining-room I wanted to run my hands on the glossy wood and along the curved arm rests and be served from the great green and white dish that sat in the middle of the table on a lace mat.

My wish was fulfilled but not in the fashion that I had envisaged, on the evening in August when my dream bubble burst. I had floated through Cecelia's birthday supper, the glow in my heart and fevered brain matching the flaring blush of the candles. Everyone seemed witty and carefree; Ivan snapping his bread briskly, Wilhelm, drunk and merry, passing me the serving dish with elaborate gallantry while Beatrice enthused about her jewellery classes, her glowing cigarette never far from her lips, Leandra saying she had been a bridesmaid five times and hoped one day to be a bride, Luca acting the perfect, genial host, Cecelia smiling on us all, speaking faster as the champagne and wine worked their charms.

I'll never forget Cecelia's face that evening; she had the

49

same expression that I saw that day in the photograph, a smile filled with the sparkle of expectation, eyes that glowed with love.

4

We soon established a routine at Dauncey Court. Bres was an early riser, always up at the crack of dawn – he said that this was a legacy from the days when he was a baker and had to get the dough going. He rang a little bell outside my door at eight and I dragged myself up, making an effort for him that I refused my mother. We breakfasted together on cereal and toast with his homemade dark orange marmalade or almond croissants warm from the deli-catessen nearby. Bres would have been out and about 'taking the morning air', buying his newspaper, chatting with other caretakers at the many blocks of flats in the area, sometimes stopping for a Turkish coffee to kick start the morning. If the weather was bad he would spend a while on his painting in progress, a view from the famous Derry city walls towards the guildhall.

While we ate Bres wrote his list of tasks for the day in a small red notebook, using a pencil he kept tucked behind his ear. He had large, firm handwriting and formed a rounded A, the kind you find in Celtic manuscripts. His list always involved electricians, plumbers, renovators, decorators or carpenters. Buildings were like people, he explained: as they got older they needed constant and kindly maintenance. He himself was in this phase of his life, having crowns fitted on teeth, swallowing blood-pressure medication and attending physiotherapy for the arthritis in his left knee. The latter, he claimed, was a consequence of playing Gaelic football in his youth. There would also be jobs to do like the laundry or *dhobi*, as Bres called it. He had used a number of such phrases since his army days; times of arrival or departure were referred to as *ETA* and *ETD*, if anyone was late he would wonder if they had gone *AWOL*, putting a stop to anything was *putting the kibosh* on it and preparations for going anywhere were *getting the kit tickety-boo*.

Every morning when I woke I remembered all over again that my father was dead. The knowledge was like a cruel blade that persistently sliced anew into my tender brain. It was particularly grim on those mornings when I had been aware of my father in that half-sleep just before waking, felt him real and near. I would lie and picture us walking in parkland or woods, as we frequently did, with him naming the trees, plants and wild flowers for me. From an early age I could spot a blue thimble flower, lady's tresses, rough hawksbeard and early marsh orchid and I would sketch the ones that I found most beautiful or whose names tickled me: ragged robin, sticky mouse-ear, goat's rue. As the awful realization stabbed into me once more I would roll into a foetal curl and squeeze my eyes tight, trying to summon the imaginary world again. I had kept one of his jumpers that smelled of him, a scent of soap, school dust and warm grass. It was tucked under my mattress and I would take it out and bury my face in it.

Sometimes, when I glanced at Bres, I was startled by a glimpse of my father; there was the same wistful smile, stray wisp of hair on the forehead, the same habit of folding the arms and rocking back thoughtfully on the back legs of a chair. At breakfast, my father had been accustomed to reading out snippets from the paper, absent-mindedly dripping marmalade as he regaled us with another political scandal. *Just listen to this!* he would say, tapping the page crossly with his toast. His reading aloud used to enrage my mother, who complained that the newspaper was ruined for her by the time she got to it, as well as covered in crumbs and butter; if it ever came to divorce, she stated, it would count as daily cruelty. At times, when Bres was pondering over his list, thinking aloud, I would have to look away, squeezing my crossed arms tight. He must have sensed my anguish; as he sugared his last cup of coffee I would feel his hand lightly patting mine.

I was responsible for washing up after breakfast and sometimes arranging lunch: sandwiches, soup, scrambled eggs and such. Other than that and turning up for an evening meal at seven, I was free to do as I liked as long as I let Bres know my general scheme of manoeuvres for the day. Every night, as I was going to bed, he would say: *time for lights out; there's another day done and dusted.*

I spent my first days at Dauncey Court exploring the area. I had a little rucksack in which I packed my sketchbook and a couple of apples. I felt intrepid as I marched along the streets, around Orange Square with its antique emporiums and restaurants and past the statue of the boy Mozart who had lived in a house opposite the square for a brief period in childhood. Then up to Sloane Square, noting the dozens of blue plaques testifying to the fondness that writers, artists and actors had always had for the area and down the King's Road as far as World's End, a name that I loved; how wonderful to go out and be able to say, *I'm going to World's End*. I turned through to the Fulham Road and along to South Kensington and the delights of the museums. The moment when I spied the tall spires of the Natural History Museum never failed to thrill me. In the Victoria and Albert I stared at the Great Bed of Ware and lingered over the ornate embellishments of Chinese furniture.

Those London streets became my therapy, pricking my preoccupied bubble, gradually allowing me to experience the living world as real again. No one impinged on me; I could move, breathe and observe, adjust to the new rhythms of the traffic, the bustle and then sudden peace of the many unexpected backwaters. I walked my grief, tired it out, let the sun and breeze assuage it. Now and again I stopped and gripped my fists tight, turning my face, pretending to study a plaque, a shop window or a beautiful gateway. Nobody noticed or bothered me or offered unwanted solace. Slowly, very slowly, I felt a hint of ease in my heart, the sharp pain becoming a duller ache.

The streets fascinated me. I noticed the huge numbers of cleaning women beating doormats, mopping steps and watering plants, the nannies pushing strollers, small children attached to their wrists with bright-blue safety leads. They were all tiny, fine-boned women, brown-skinned, dressed in trousers and tabards, dark hair neatly gripped. Their charges were almost all blonde, kitted out in designer wear, skins glowing with the bloom of healthy youth. The women nodded at me as I passed but they looked distracted. Sometimes they would stop and converse with each other in fast, tonal languages. I thought they sounded angry but guessed it was just the speed and intonation of their speech that made them seem that way.

I noticed, too, how amazingly rubbish-free the streets were and how much maintenance went into keeping them that way. There was an army of litter-pickers and street-cleaning vehicles, small, barrel-shaped objects with swishing brushes scouring the gutters and kerbs. Men wearing orange-and-yellow jackets sometimes leapt from these machines and wielded jet sprays on the pavements. I even saw them propped on hydraulic ladders, cleaning the street signs, teasing the grime from individual letters. Bres said that wealth had a kind of glow or sheen to it and that money looked after money. I began to see what he meant as I compared this affluent corner of London to my typically tatty suburban sprawl.

One sweltering afternoon, hiking along Chester Row, I glanced through the open door of a majestic Georgian house, the kind with a narrow frontage, railings and steps to the pavement. A naked man was standing and yawning, scratching his head with one hand, holding a phone in the other. We looked at each other simultaneously, both startled. I hurried on, astonished, blushing. I turned a corner and started to laugh. I hadn't seen a naked man in the flesh before; I hadn't realized there would be quite so much hair and muscle and sheer immediacy. I closed my eyes for a moment, capturing the image. He had also been beautiful. That evening I drew him from memory, the curve of back and buttocks, the fuzzy shadow of pubic hair, the furry covering on his arms. I tore the drawing up when I had finished, suddenly feeling uncomfortably warm and like a peeping Tom. I walked past the house again on a couple of occasions but the door was always closed. I wondered if I would recognize him if I met him in the street and if he would still look beautiful clothed.

The riches of the streets were almost equalled by the riches of the gardens at Dauncey Court. Using my key, I ventured into them in the early evenings at first, when none of the residents used them. (According to Bres, as soon as the sun was over the yardarm they were too busy at their drinks cabinets, mixing their first gin and tonic – except of course for Sylvia Leycroft, who mixed her first at breakfast.) I was saving the gardens up for proper exploration as soon as I had finished my orientation exercise in the neighbourhood. I found them mysterious, peaceful and romantic. Looking back, I can see that their exquisiteness lay in their lush maturity and their slightly neglected air. The residents visited them only occasionally; Luca and his friends probably made the most use of them, particularly late at night for what they jokingly referred to as their 'garden parties'. There was the odd social function, someone's birthday or anniversary and, when the Chelsea Flower show was on, members of a local horticultural group were allowed to visit.

The knowledge my father had passed on meant that I knew many of the abundant plants and flowers as well as their Latin and common names; the masses of tiny yellow *anethum*, the pinkish pompom-shaped *cirsium*, the vibrant crimson, yellow and purple intensely scented stock – my father had called them the show-offs of the garden –

the blue and orange bird of paradise, delicate spikes of veronica, papery love-in-the-mist, marigolds and snapdragons. They formed an elegant drift of colours, heavenly scents and shapes that seemed to me like a dream landscape.

There were three ponds; the largest was the bog-garden pond, which had a rockery above and a series of shallower ponds around it, then came the water lily pond and the smallest, the forget-me-not pond. It was the last of these that became my favourite, with its tiny white and blue flowers, bordered by lady's smock, marsh marigolds and willowherb. A large toad lived by the forget-me-not pond. I made his regular acquaintance as I sat and sketched or read and sometimes we would look at each other for minutes at a time until he crawled away.

Gina, the gardener who came in three times a week, was impressed by my knowledge and was keen to point out her rarer successes, such as glory lilies and heliconia. Gina was particularly proud of her tub of Queen Victoria's myrtle; the myrtle, she informed me, had come from a sprig from the royal wedding bouquet given to one of her bridesmaids by the Queen and handed on through Gina's great-aunt. Gina was a vague, middle-aged woman with a plump torso and muscular arms and legs; a faded hippy type in batik-print tops and well-washed jeans, who believed in allowing nature room to breathe and develop. She would tell me this as she embraced a tree, throwing her arms around its sturdy trunk. So there were overgrown corners, bog garden, damp, untended grasses and untrimmed hedges for birds to nest and where foxes, hedgehogs and mice could live secret lives. She allowed leaves to rot where they fell, kept a large compost heap and refused to use insecticides. Bird-feeders hung from tree branches and trunks. Gina's environmental fervour would be very much in vogue now; Bres thought she was a little batty. He would have preferred manicured gardens like the ones in magazines; lawns mown with fine precision and regimented plants, but he couldn't interfere with Gina because she was related to the aristocratic family who owned the land and most of the properties around Dauncey Court.

It was in the gardens that I first met Luca. I was sitting in the shade on a bench in mid-afternoon, sketching a bronze statue of Pan that stood on a plinth by the forget-me-not pond. The day was hot and still. I had kicked off my sandals and was enjoying the soft grass under my toes. Water boat-men were skimming the pond and bees drifted over the roses. I heard a soft whistling and looked up to see a tall man walking in my direction, holding an instrument, like a guitar but smaller. He was wearing jeans, a tight white T-shirt and open-toed sandals, the kind with one loop of leather around the big toe. As he came nearer I saw that he had hairy arms – thick, dark hairs, and a complicated-looking watch with various buttons and dials, the kind that my father couldn't afford but would ponder over wistfully in magazines.

'Greetings,' he said. 'You must be the caretaker's grand-daughter.'

'That's right. Hello.'

He bowed. 'I am Luca Gonzi, friend of Cecelia. She is coming down soon, to take a stroll.' He had an accent, although his English was perfect.

'Are you Italian?'

'No, but you've guessed the right area. I am Maltese,

from near Valletta.'

'I've never met anyone from Malta before,' I told him. 'My name is Martina but I'm called Marti.'

'It suits you. Short, to the point. Little Marti; yes!'

He sounded amused. I wasn't sure if he was referring to my stature so I looked down and examined my pencil. He put a foot on the bench beside me, rested the instrument across his thigh. He had large, square toenails, clean and well-shaped, with perfect crescents.

'You want to be an artist?'

'I don't know. I like to draw.'

'Let me see.' He leaned forward, very close and turned my sketch pad round. 'Very good, I think. You have talent.' He spoke with confidence and precision: a man who expected to be heard.

'Thanks. Are you a musician?'

'Yes, I play many stringed instruments; guitar, mandolin, lute.' He gestured at the instrument he was holding, tapped its rounded body. 'The harpsichord is also in my repertoire and I sing. My voice coach says that I have professional potential. Would you like me to sing for you?'

I was taken aback but he didn't notice; he wasn't waiting for an answer. He sat right beside me on the bench, making it shudder, and strummed what I now understood to be a lute, frowning slightly, tightening a peg. He began to sing in a powerful baritone about a nightingale, in a style that was unfamiliar to me. I only knew that it must be from an earlier century:

. . . The nightingale, so soon as April bringeth, so soon as April bringeth, so soon as April bringeth

unto her rested sense a perfect waking, sings out
her woes, a thorn her songbook making. . . .

His eyes were closed. He sounded wistful, caught up in
his story. I was fascinated, watching his firm red lips and his
confident fingers on the strings. I felt as if I had gone to
sleep and woken up in an altered world where I might see
women in full-skirted gowns and men wearing hose and
ruffs. As he finished there was a sound of clapping; I looked
up and there was Cecelia standing on a balcony, her stick
hooked over one arm.

' "Is it not strange that sheep's guts should hale souls out
of men's bodies?" ' She called. 'Bravo, a sublime rendition,
Luca.'

He leapt up, strode to below the balcony and made her
a deep bow, then flung an arm up in a dramatic pose, a
muscular Romeo to her ageing Juliet.

'Shall I climb up to you, *namrata*, and escort you down?'

She gave a little laugh and a regal wave, told him he was
a silly darling boy and that she was on her way. He watched
her close the windows behind her, swaying with the exer-
tion, then he turned back to me with a bland expression.

'Amazing', I said brightly, to break the silence.

Cecelia came towards us walking slowly, carefully, placing her stick steadily on the grass. With the sun illuminating
her slim frame, she looked ethereal. Despite the walking-
stick you could have taken her for a much younger woman
until she drew nearer and the deep lines and ravaged neck
came into focus.

Luca rose, propped his lute against a tree trunk and went
to her side, extending his arm for her to hold. She hooked

her hand through his elbow and looked up at him, smiling. Her pale-blue silk shift dress had cream oval buttons and she had a little cape in the same material around her shoulders: cream with blue piping. She wore her handbag over her arm, like the Queen. He led her to the bench and stood as she settled herself, then he sat on the grass in front of her.

'Good afternoon, Martina,' she said, nodding to me. 'Are you well?'

'Yes, thanks. I enjoyed the song.'

'Song! My goodness, *The Nightingale* is a madrigal, by Sir Philip Sidney. Far more than a song, you know. A lyrical poem set to music.'

I had never knowingly heard a madrigal before, although I knew the type of music from watching a film about Elizabeth I. 'It's lovely,' I said feebly.

Luca made an elegant gesture with his hand towards Cecelia. 'Do you know, little Marti, that I am an incredibly lucky man? I have been fortunate enough to find this beautiful lady to be my patron. Many artists have not been so blessed and their talent has withered. It was written in the stars, I think.'

'There are things that are meant to be,' Cecelia affirmed, gazing at him. 'I do believe that fate brought us together.'

'My grandfather always says that about himself and my grandmother,' I told her. 'The day they met he was supposed to go to the races, but he went to a dance instead and there she was, pouring the lemonade. Their families didn't approve but they were determined to be together. They eloped and got married. When they returned, they drove around town in an open horse-drawn

61

carriage so that *everyone* would know they *were* together. My grandmother had *Love Conquers All* engraved in her wedding ring.'

'Well . . .' Cecelia said. She looked at me quizzically and laughed. I felt as if I had passed some kind of test. 'How quirky and courageous, I suppose. And you are sketching Pan on this fine afternoon?'

'Yes.'

Cecelia unclasped her bag, slowly drew out a tiny pair of glasses and set them on her nose. She looked at my drawing, peering closely. I could smell wine on her breath. I felt cornered.

'You have a gift,' she observed, looking from the drawing to me. 'And the subject you have chosen – you know about Pan?'

'He's a Greek god.'

'Good, yes. He represents physicality, all things animal. I suppose that's why he is so often found in gardens, with his reed pipes. That isn't a particularly good statue, though. There was a beautifully formed one on a hotel terrace on Crete, I recall. Pan is rather dissolute, though; maybe not a subject for a young girl, but then I'm old-fashioned about such things, aren't I, Luca?'

'You have good judgement, Cecelia. I think for little Marti he is a useful subject to practise on during a warm afternoon, yes?'

I nodded.

'And what have you been doing with yourself on these fine days?' Cecelia asked.

'Going to museums, exploring, helping Bres.'

'Bres?'

'My grandfather.'

Cecelia winced as if I had dug my pencil into her. 'What an extraordinary name to call him. Not very dignified for a man of his age. What did you call your grandfather, Luca?'

'Nannu.'

'Oh, that's much more seemly, yes.'

I couldn't see why. It struck me that despite her upper-class drawl, her fine clothes, style and expensive-smelling perfume, she could be impolite. She adjusted her cape, patting the edges and put her glasses back in their case, fumbling with the hinge. She had a little tremble in her fingers, a fussy movement.

'When does Wilhelm arrive?' she asked Luca.

'Tomorrow afternoon, *namrata*. I thought we might eat out in the evening, L'Auberge Cerise, maybe?' He knelt up and straightened the hem of her skirt.

She tapped her hands together. 'Oh yes, let's. It was awfully good there last time and the service is so discreet. I shall wear my lemon cashmere if it's back from the cleaners.'

'I picked it up this morning. Good, I'll book a table.' He sat back on his heels, looked up at her consideringly. 'I think you should go to the hairdresser tomorrow, Cecelia. Just a little tinting needed around the ears. And time for a manicure, too.'

'Will you ring for me, darling boy?'

'Of course.'

'Oh, what would I do without my Luca? Now, will you sing once more; a Scottish song . . . dear Robbie Burns?'

Luca raised his lute, leaned his head close to it as he strummed chords, adjusting strings. Then he rested one foot against the bench and sang in a good imitation of a Scots accent.

Ye banks and braes o' bonnie Doon,
How can ye bloom sae fresh and fair?
How can ye chant, ye little birds,
And I sae weary, full o' care!
Thou'll break my heart, thou warbling bird,
That wantons thro' the flowering thorn!
Thou mind me o' departed joys,
Departed, never to return.

I listened to the sweetly sad lyrics and lilting tune, my chest suddenly tight with misery and longing. Luca looked at me and stood straight in one fluid action.

'Maybe it is too sad a song for a sunny day, little Marti is becoming pensive. I will save the second verse for later, when there are evening shadows and gloom is more at home. Our friend will want to get on with her work in progress and we had better move if we are going to make Harley Street and back before my singing lesson.' He hung his lute across his body like a troubadour.

'Goodness, yes.' Cecelia balanced her stick and got up carefully, smoothing her skirt.

She said good afternoon to me again, formally, and as they moved away, her hand linked again through his arm, I heard her say, 'I'm so looking forward to meeting Wilhelm after everything you've told me.' I tried to carry on with my sketch but I couldn't regain my concentration, my mind dwelling on departed joys. I shook my head and thought of Cecelia's social plans. I wondered what the lemon

cashmere looked like and what it would be like to experience discreet service at L'Auberge Cerise. I imagined dim
lighting, leather chairs and snowy table-linen with waiters
as shadowy figures gliding silently. In the end I closed my
book and lay on my stomach, peering into the mysterious,
reedy depths of the pond, wondering if I might spot any
underwater life. I whispered to a busy water boatman that I
would give anything to collect frogspawn with my father
just one more time.

I decided that this was going to be a summer of
Experiences. Life had thrown a strange and hideous thing
my way but, as my father often said, *you've got to ride the
surf when it's rough*. Once, when I had been bullied by a
gigantic, bossy girl at school in Bristol, I had moaned to him
that I didn't know what I should do, how I should behave.
Tapping his teeth with his red Biro (I had interrupted him
when he was marking) he had advised that the rule of
thumb in every situation was to be oneself. I had gone away
and stared in the mirror, trying to decide who I was, not
realizing that it is the question that dogs everyone throughout life, not just in childhood. I had ended up in London
because he had died. Well, I couldn't have him back and if,
as everyone told me, he lived on in me, I would try to
embark on this adventure with an enquiring mind, which
was being myself, as far as I knew.

I liked Gina, the gardener. She was matey but not conde-
scending. She was a vegetarian and brought sandwiches
and pasties wrapped in greaseproof paper to eat during her
breaks, made with things I'd never tasted before; feta
cheese, bulgur wheat and artichokes. She'd tear off little

sections and offer them to me if she found me sketching. Then I would put my work down and we would chat. I found her hard to follow sometimes; she leapt from one topic of conversation to another in her stuttery voice, looping back unexpectedly to a subject from ten minutes previously. Her hair was thick and straggly, with a zigzag parting that seemed as crazy as her verbal meanderings. (When I commented on her conversational style to Bres he snorted and said, *hmm, probably too many drugs in the sixties*.)

It was Gina who told me about the differences between old and new money, a concept unfamiliar to me. She had asked me whom I'd met in the flats and when I told her, she explained that Cecelia was old money because she came from an established family who had been rich since the eighteenth century and that Philip Courteney was new money because he had inherited from his mother whose wealth came from American oil in the nineteen fifties.

'What about Sylvie Leycroft?'

'Hmm, she's difficult . . . new money, squandered, I suppose. The arts don't really fit the spectrum, though, they're out there somewhere on their own.'

'So what are you?' I asked, chewing, unsure whether I liked goat's cheese, which had a whiff of pee and reminded me of the aroma the twins sometimes left behind in a room.

'Oh, old money, but very little of it,' Gina replied. 'My dad was the youngest and made daft investments with his portion. Humphrey – my cousin – he owns Dauncey and the other properties – he pays me over the odds to do the gardens in all his places. Decent of him, really and just as well as I'm not qualified to do anything much and I have to earn a crust somehow. Cecelia has never worked in her life but she's got her trust fund and shares galore, so it's never mattered, and her husband was rich in his own right. Some get all the jam and others get scrapings from the jar.'

I liked that saying. Gina didn't sound at all bitter, just matter of fact. She leaned back on her elbows and looked up at the sky.

'I must get to the podiatrist,' she said, lifting one bare grubby foot and staring at it. 'I've got a corn that's killing me. Mind you, one of the problems for Cecelia with having all that jam means that some people come along and dig a big spoon in.'

'You mean Luca?' I'd decided that I didn't like feta cheese and I was stretching one hand behind me, casually crumbling what was left around a clump of sweet william.

'The lovely Luca and his "friends", too. Different pals of his turn up regularly. Cecelia loves it all, laps it up while they eat her food, drink her booze and get her to pay at fancy restaurants. It makes her feel young and in the swim of things. Still, she can do what she wants with her money, including forking out for major refurbishments. Luca's been bending her ear about his room not being big enough so they've got a grand scheme under way for knocking through and soundproofing, all sorts. I think I heard a Jacuzzi mentioned. You've got to hand it to Luca, he does-n't do anything in half-measures and he is undoubtedly the apple of her eye. We all have a fatal flaw and Cecelia's is that she believes utterly in romance.'

'Have you got a fatal flaw?'

Gina put the soles of her feet together, tailor pose. 'Oh yes, definitely. I never expect enough.'

'I suppose I'm too young to know what mine is.'

'Yes, the realization comes, if it does, with age, after you've cocked up a few times.'

I passed her my can of lemonade and she took a deep swig, coughed and burped loudly. I wasn't sure I wanted it back after that.

'Thanks. I think one of the honeysuckles has a virus, I must get some advice. Does your grandfather know anything about climbers?'

'I shouldn't think so, he's never been interested in gardens much.'

'Funny that, and he comes from the Emerald Isle, with all that greenery. I'm sure he must have some idea.'

She'd lost me there. To my knowledge, Bres preferred gardens seen through windows and the only turf that concerned him was on racecourses. Gina swore suddenly, crouched forward and lunged under a clump of bright-blue veronica.

'Look!' she said, dragging out an empty cigarette packet and a wine bottle. 'I've told Luca about leaving rubbish here, he takes no bloody notice, laughs in my face.'

'How do you know it's him?'

'Him or one of his friends, they use the garden after dark for their recreation. Creatures of the night. Look at the wine: Chateau Haut Brion, 1953. We're not talking bargain bin, it's from Cecelia's store.'

I examined the sepia-and-white label, sniffed the rich aroma of the bottle, turning it to read the description: *the wine is extremely soft, revealing considerable amber and rust at the edge, but it still possesses rich, creamy fruit and medium to full body.*

'Mark my words, he's getting cocky, he'll go too far one of these days,' Gina said, crumpling the cigarette packet in her strong hand.

5

Bres was a gregarious and big-hearted man who loved company. His flat was never silent; even when he was on his own and painting, he had the radio on or listened to something from his vast music collection. He couldn't walk down a street without striking up at least one conversation, usually with a total stranger. He would set out to go to the corner shop and come back two hours later, saying that he'd helped a tourist who couldn't find his way to the train, come across a pregnant woman fainting by the railings of the park, assisted a chap whose motorbike had broken down or simply got chatting to someone who turned out to have a fascinating life history involving bigamy or torture or mistaken identity. Whenever people remarked on his sociability he'd say: *the grave's a fine and private place, but none, I think, do there embrace*, which certainly silenced the commentator.

He had a set of male friends which he had accumulated over the years and during his varied occupations. Like him, they all had nicknames which seemed to be a kind of pass-word for their boys' club, and they too had led eventful lives. I already knew Righty Mitchell, who was left-handed. He'd been at school with Bres and turned up at all our family occasions. The others I met at Dauncey Court for the first time one Thursday evening, which was their regular arrangement with Bres for a session of Guinness and beef casserole followed by card-playing. There was Tullamore Joe who had fled the old IRA after a falling-out, Eppo, who survived a heart attack even though medics had pronounced him dead, the Bishop, a refugee from Uganda, Fatso Flanagan, who was, of course, rake-thin and had lost a leg in a rail accident and Guevara, who had escaped on the last plane out of Cuba before Castro took power. They all smoked cigarettes or cigars except for Eppo, who favoured a pipe with cherry tobacco, so I saw them through a kind of misty haze when I came into the living-room. Bres had pulled out the dining table and they were crowded around its extended width, the orange casserole dish brimming with its beery load, accompanied by a big plate of potatoes; it was like the smokers' last supper.

They all stood when I came in, which made me feel slightly regal, and Guevara took my hand and kissed it. I was seated between Guevara and Fatso Flanagan, who insisted on trying to find the juiciest pieces of beef for me and advised me to have more of the carrots because I was a growing girl. The Bishop, who was so called because he had once had leanings to the priesthood, tapped his knife on the table and insisted on grace before we tucked in. Bres threw down the oven gloves, raised his eyes heavenwards and sat with his arms folded while the Bishop said: 'Thanks to the man upstairs for the great grub and may he look kindly on my aces tonight.' Eppo observed that this sounded blasphemous and Tullamore Joe said that it was the kind of ingratiating prayer that could go against you if you weren't careful. When I added that this could especially be the case if the fella upstairs happened to be a female who hated cards, Bres threw me an approving look and said, 'that's the girl!'

Righty Mitchell had been party to my grandparents' elopement and acted as a witness at their wedding. His own wife had run off with another man six months after their marriage and he had lived on his own ever since. Bres was fond of him, even though he was a bit of a bore who liked the sound of his own monotonous voice, and made sure to include him in any social activities. He was a painter on building sites and big projects; he had once painted Tower Bridge. He didn't look strong enough for such work with his skinny neck and waiflike appearance. His hair and fingernails were always ingrained with shreds of the industrial paint he applied, mainly a grey-cream, salt and pepper combination which rendered him prematurely aged. He rested his chin on his hands, looking at me.

'Did I ever tell you about your love-struck granda?' he asked me, a huge grin on his face.

My heart sank. Only about a thousand times since I was in my cradle, I thought, nodding at him. A groan went round the table. Righty, of course, was oblivious to this and the deep enjoyment he derived from recounting his tally of stories made the most jaundiced listener adopt an expression of forbearance.

'The night he met your grandmother, he came round to our house, hunkered down on his knees by the fire and said, "I've met her, I've met a great wee girl. She's the one!" But then his father said he was too young to marry, declared he should wait five year. Five year! There was such a to-do! Your granda took to his bed and said he wouldn't come out of it till his father changed his mind, but your gran sent him a note saying she missed him too much and he was to shift out of his pit and do something. So in the heel of the hunt, him and me and your gran took off to Belfast, bought a ring and caught the train to Dublin. Your gran had made us chicken sandwiches and they were the best I ever tasted. We were worried but she was laughing all the way, she was a great one for larks and adventures. We had ice creams on O'Connell street even though it was November; the taste was terrific.'

He sat back smiling, shaking his head as if it was the first time he'd told the story and picked a sliver of paint from his thumb. 'I'd say, Marti, that you'll maybe be a small woman, like your grandmother.'

'Not at all,' Bres snorted. 'She's small now but she'll put on a spurt later in her teens, like I did. She's just biding her time, conserving her energy.'

I was pleased at that because I wanted to be tall; I had read that tall people were taken more notice of in life and commanded better salaries.

'I told Cecelia about your and grandma's elopement,' I informed Bres. 'She thought it was truly romantic. She says that one of the awful things about modern life is that romance has died. When her husband was wooing her, he sent her a dozen red roses every morning and all the years they were married, he presented her with a flower corsage for dinner at night.'

Guevara snorted. 'She thinks she's found romance again

now, anyway, with her Latin crooner. As they say, there's no fool like an old fool.'

Eppo nodded. 'I don't suppose Mr Gonzi gives her many flowers; the gifts mainly go in the other direction.'

'He brought her some this evening,' I said, 'a great bunch of freesias, highly scented.'

'Well,' Bres said, helping himself to more casserole, 'there's one thing you can be sure of under the heavens; the money he bought them with came from her own purse.'

I had just come from Cecelia's, where I had been invited in the late afternoon for tea. A vellum card in a cream envelope had arrived that morning, with Cecelia's name and address printed on the top in bold italic lettering and the request in her own elegant, spidery handwriting: *Cecelia Buchanan requests the pleasure of Miss Martina Breslin's company for tea at 4.30 p.m. today.* I'd scrutinized the card, admiring the quality of the paper and the script in navy-blue ink. When I held it close and sniffed it, it smelled a little dusty, as if it might have lain in a box for some time. I had never received such a formal, classy invitation and I propped it on the mantelpiece because that's what they did in old films. Bres had read it, said I must have made an impression and I'd better make sure I crooked my little finger when I was sipping from my teacup and not slurp as I drank. I had made an effort by putting on my white jeans and a clean blue T-shirt and coiling my hair into a little knot which I thought made me seem taller and older.

The door was open when I arrived, with two workmen

carrying through a ladder and boxes of tools. Thick plastic sheeting had been placed on the hall carpet and I could hear Cecelia laying the law down about how they were to take care not to do any damage and that she had no wish to hear their radio playing. She saw me and waved me in as she informed them that refreshments were *not* available on the premises.

'Good afternoon, Martina. Such a bore, having these chaps in, making noise and fuss and they seem to have been here forever. But there, omelettes cannot be made without eggs being broken and it will create a much better living space for Luca. It really is a rather lovely project we've planned; he will in effect have his own apartment within the larger accommodation. I've always found making plans so energizing and he's so excited, especially about the Jacuzzi. He needs to relax his muscles, you know; they become very tense with all the rehearsing, particularly around the neck and shoulders. The warmth will be so soothing.'

'Is a bit of whistling acceptable, lady?' one of the men asked mildly.

Cecelia gave him a stern look. 'If you must, you may whistle softly.'

Luca was out so it was just Cecelia and myself with Daphne shadowing us and leaping on and off furniture whenever she thought Cecelia wasn't paying her enough attention. I was glad that I had showered and changed because Cecelia was looking terrifically chic in a heavy silk black-and-white striped sheath dress with a necklace of glistening jet beads. Her hair had been done differently, no longer in a pleat but coiled in a fashion like my own except it was much more expertly accomplished and encircled with a grey scarf that matched her dress fabric. When she let me in she took me to her bedroom, saying that there was something she wanted to show me.

'I do think you'll appreciate my collection, with your artist's eye,' she said, opening the door to a room I hadn't entered on my previous tour.

It was a huge room overlooking one side of the garden and the statue of Pan where I had first met Luca. The balcony outside the French windows was the one she had stood on the day he sang the madrigal. It was decorated with bright yellows and whites and acres of swagged gold-velvet curtains at the tall windows. There was a king-size bed covered in cushions and magazines, with an oyster-coloured silk dressing gown draped across the end. One of those little tables that you can pull across a bed stood beside it and I pictured Cecelia having her breakfast there, propped up on her plump pillows and reading a magazine, like a film star. An open door in the corner led to an ensuite bathroom. There were so many yellow and white flowers, I felt overwhelmed with the sight and scent.

Cecelia led me to an oval table on which stood a collection of beautiful bottles, all shapes, sizes and colours: deep sea-blues and turquoises, vibrant reds, pinks and lilacs, with scrolls, curlicues, engravings and frostings. She was pleased at my intake of breath.

'Now, first of all,' she said, 'do you know what kind of table this is?'

Apart from highly polished dark wood, I had no idea and I confessed as much.

She folded her arms and scrutinized me. 'Hmm, well, Martina, if you are going to develop your talent, you need to learn to appreciate the quality of things. This is a rosewood jewellery table, circa 1835. A beautiful piece of craftsmanship. This beaded edging is called ormolu and the legs, with their slender outward curve, are cabriole. This gracious table suitably displays my prize collection of scent bottles. I've been building it for over twenty years. I started in Paris with this Lalique, and I suppose it became something of an obsession, like all collections.' She held up the Lalique, a slim, delicate item of clear and frosted glass with a green patina.

'Can I touch it?' I asked.

'Yes, you can hold it very carefully.'

It was cool and light, the green a shade of young spring leaves or budding ferns. She took it back from me after a moment, setting it carefully in its place and continued pointing and explaining.

'This one with amethyst and a blue morning glory decoration is Thomas Webb cameo glass, this with the bulbous shape in turquoise and opaline is a mid nineteenth century Palais Royal, this Victorian cut-glass teal green was a very special find in Munich, this pair with the lovely floral spray motif are Val St Lambert and this – now this is rare and unusual, a Salviati double-lipped . . . oh, and look at this, with the chinoiserie motif, it's early Bohemian.'

'They're astonishing, I've never seen such things close up before. Are they worth a fortune?'

'A good amount, especially the eighteenth-century Czech ones. My lawyer wants me to keep them in a lockable cabinet but that would spoil my pleasure, having to look at them through a pane of glass. What's the point in having things of such beauty if I can't touch them and enjoy them?'

I stood, gazing.

'There's something so charming and graceful about them,' Cecelia said, 'the refraction of the light, the beauty of the lines and curves. Even the more ornate ones have a stylish simplicity.'

'Have you got a favourite?'

'I change my mind every week. At the moment, the Salviati, I think; the coiling lips resemble swans' necks. Would you sketch one or two for me?'

'I don't know if I could,' I said doubtfully, 'they're so intricate. I could try.'

'Super, we'll arrange it.' She moved one bottle with a dolphin-shaped stopper a fraction to the right, then to the left, then held her hands over the top of the collection as if blessing them.

'Time for tea now, I think. Would you mind awfully helping me make it? Fortunata, my maid, only works in the mornings. She's a gem and she used to come all day but Luca and I found it intrusive in the end, having the help around all the time. One needs it when one is on one's own but with Luca here, the mornings are sufficient.'

I followed her to the kitchen, thinking that she was a person I would have expected to be in awe of: someone completely outside my usual social circles. Yet I felt at ease with her, intrigued by her. I put this thought aside, to reflect on later. On a kitchen worktop was a lacquered tray laid with a tea service in white china with little rose-buds; two cups and saucers, a bowl of thin lemon slices, a jug of milk, a silver tea-strainer and holder, sugar lumps in an oval dish with a silver tongs and a plate of tiny smoked salmon sandwiches, covered with a white napkin. The tea was Darjeeling and under Cecelia's instruction, I warmed the china pot and scooped the huge leaves from a Harrods tin, pouring the water just as it boiled.

'It smells so delicate,' I said. 'I've never tasted Darjeeling.'

'I think it is the prince of teas,' Cecelia told me. 'Closely followed by Keemun, which I prefer last thing at night. Can you be a sweetie and carry that through? There is a trolley thing but it's such a fuss. We'll go to the drawing-room, it catches the afternoon sun.'

'No problem,' I said, lifting the tray and steadying my nerves as I thought of the possible value of the tea service I was holding. Cecelia walked slowly ahead of me while I tried to stop the tray trembling. She wasn't using her stick and she held a piece of furniture now and again as she made her way along the hallway.

Cecelia poured the tea, making a bit of a mess because of the tremor in her hands. She told me to help myself to sandwiches and I did, taking several as they were so small.

'These are delicious,' I said, munching. There was a herby mayonnaise layer under the salmon and the bread was soft and light. I expected it all came from Harrods or Fortnum's.

'Good, I'm glad you like them, Fortunata does them particularly well now. When she first came to me, she knew nothing at all about English food, she drenched everything in oil and pepper. I had to talk her through some simple dishes.' She cut a tiny morsel from one of the sandwiches and placed it in her mouth.

'I would have thought you'd like foreign food,' I said, 'if you've travelled a lot.'

'Oh, when in Rome one does as a Roman, but I have always liked good, traditional English fare. Frankly, I have little appetite these days. As one gets older, one's need for food diminishes. Most people eat too much, that's why there is so much ghastly obesity about. You are slim, Martina. Your figure is very similar to my own at your age.'

'I'm always hungry and I'm always eating,' I confessed, eyeing the remaining sandwiches. 'I don't know how I stay thin; my grandfather says I have hollow legs. He also says I have an appetite like a bird: a vulture.'

'But that is quite as it should be, you are storing the goodness and burning energy, working to emerge from a chrysalis into, I would guess, a stunning young woman.' She smiled vaguely, feeding salmon to Daphne, who had jumped on to her lap, tail arched. I watched Daphne's pink tongue lick the fish, then snatch it greedily. 'And I believe your father died recently?' she said, as if it was a natural subject to follow dietary matters.

I was taken aback but I supposed that Bres had mentioned it to her when he explained that I was coming to stay. I gripped my teacup with both hands. 'Yes, in a car crash.'

'I am so very sorry. I see where you are carrying your grief, on your shoulders, pinching at you. It's a weary weight to have to bear when you are young. Now, do get down Daphne, you're becoming a bore and you'll make yourself sick.' She shooed the cat and it jumped lightly down, circling her chair before it sprang on to the window ledge and bathed in a pool of sun, paws stretched ahead, blinking.

We both watched Daphne for a moment or two. Then Cecelia sat back in her chair and sighed.

'Tell me, Martina, do you wonder if your father thought about you as he was dying?'

I stared; how did she know? Did she know too that again and again I'd heard the shriek of the brakes and slam of metal against metal, smelt the petrol and burning tyres, felt the thump of impact? I sat back too. There was something about Daphne's enigmatic composure and Cecelia's pleasant coolness that made the conversation effortless.

'Yes, often. In a way, I hope he died without really know-ing what was happening – that's what the police said. But then I want him to have – oh, I don't know. . . .'

'To have sent you some love as he left you?'

I nodded. It was a relief to have it named. The sun was on Cecelia's face, cruelly illuminating her wrinkles but also softening her haughty expression. She tapped the arms of her chair.

'My mother died when I was ten, drowned. I used to worry about her panic and pain as she fought the pull of the sea, but most of all I wanted her to have thought of me. I had no care for anyone else, my father or her parents. There's a lot of piffle talked about families relying on each other after a death. The truth is, we all become insane for a while, cold and full of rage and hurt. The bereaved are utterly selfish but I rather think they are entitled to be. It is only when the loss recedes that they become fully human again and able to feel for others.'

I thought I understood what she was saying. It was stark and tough but it made sense, far more than Sister Tricia's sugary simplifications. For the first time, it fully dawned on me that Bres must be missing his son terribly but was looking out for everyone else and never mentioning his own grief.

'I'm sorry about your mother,' I said.

'Thank you. We weren't close but . . . her going left a strange vacuum. A door that bangs shut in a sharp wind.'

'I don't really believe that my father is dead. I mean, I know it but I keep thinking that he'll be there when I wake up.'

'Yes. There is no comfort, except the knowledge of the love there has been. That never dies and if you have children, you will pass it on to them.'

There was a silence. Then Cecelia glanced at her watch, clicked her tongue. 'Oh, good Lord,' she said, reaching for a little box and pressing the catch. 'I've forgotten my tablets again, Luca would be so cross with me if he knew, I'm supposed to space them out properly during the day. I suppose the modern shrinks would say I'm "in denial", not wanting to admit my infirmity.' She swallowed the medication without a drink, tilting her head back. 'Speaking of Luca, where on earth has he got to? It's almost 5.30.' Smoothing her hair, she gave me a stern look. 'Have you heard people saying unpleasant things about Luca?'

'No,' I lied.

She kept looking straight at me for a few moments but seemed satisfied. 'People talk about Luca and me, the difference in our ages. I'm aware of that. I don't give a fig for any of it. He's a true soul, the salt of the earth. We met by Harrods, you know. I was trying to hail a cab in the crowds and I dropped my bag. He literally rescued me from being trodden on. We've been inseparable since. People are snobbish about him because he comes from an ordinary working-class background. They don't take the time to see his integrity, his potential.' She placed a hand against her heart.

I wasn't sure whether she thought I was one of the people who were snubbing Luca, even though she had no reason to.

'He sings really well,' I volunteered.

That brought a warm smile. 'I knew I was right about you, you have sensitivity, you are what the French call *sympathique*. I was alone and lonely when I met my dearest Luca. He brought the sun back into my life. Sometimes you know immediately when you have met a very special person. Others cannot appreciate that two people can have a loving companionship, no matter their age or class.'

That was when I told her more about Bres's elopement and how he knew straight away that he'd met 'the one'. She lit up again at the story, waxed lyrical about romance. She was attractive when she became animated, less rigid in her movements.

'Oh, you've done me good this afternoon, Martina, with your youth and energy. We must talk like this again.

Could you be a darling and make me a gin and tonic? It's all in the kitchen, by the microwave. And plenty of ice. I can use this lemon. You can take the rest of the tea things out and leave them by the sink. Fortunata will deal with them.'

I had poured wine, beer and sherry but I'd never made a gin and tonic, gin not being a drink either of my parents liked. I made my way to the kitchen, stopping to look at the work in progress in Luca's accommodation; plastering was under way in the two rooms that had been knocked into one, making a huge, light space. The bathroom had been gutted and a new floor fitted of beautiful aquamarine tiles with a mosaic pattern. Daphne came pacing along-side me as I opened the kitchen door, interested no doubt in the traces of salmon left on the serving plate. I put the plate on the floor for her to lick while I found the green bottle of gin next to some tall glasses. The tonic was in the door of the fridge and I collected an ice tray. I half-filled a glass with gin, dropped in four ice cubes and then added tonic to the brim. It fizzed, sending out a cooling spray. I sniffed and took a sip. Horrible, I thought, like watery medicine. Daphne was moving the plate across the tiles with her tongue in her desire to get every last morsel of fish. The scraping was the only sound; I listened to how quiet the flat was, reflected on the pleasure there must be in living under the same roof as other people but not having to be aware of them.

The sound of the front door opening broke my reverie. I heard Luca's voice and another man laughing, the rattle of keys as Luca put his on the silver holder in the hallway. He came into the kitchen, holding a huge bunch of pink, white and purple freesias, followed by a small man with a pony-tail.

'Hello, little Marti! Oh my, have we caught you tippling the gin?' He put the flowers down and placed his hands on his hips, grinning at me.

'It's for Cecelia, she asked me to make it.'

'Oh, of course, you came to tea today. This is my friend Wilhelm, by the way.'

Wilhelm pointed at the glasses. 'Will you make me one?' he asked, 'I love your English G and T.'

I looked at Luca, who nodded. 'I'll have one too. How about you, little Marti, are you making one for yourself?'

'No thanks, I don't drink, really. Just rosé wine, some-times.'

'Of course, you are a child, I forget because you have your serious expression, makes you seem older. Oh my God, Daphne, what are you doing?' He seized the plate from the floor, held it up to the light, examining it. 'Did you put this down?' he asked.

'Yes, there was some salmon left. . . .'

He waved a finger at me. 'You must never, never do such a thing. Do you know that this is Meissen porcelain? This plate is worth a fortune, Cecelia would faint if she knew!'

Wilhelm took the plate from him and ran his fingers around the edge, whistling soundlessly. 'Beautiful!'

'Luca, is that you? You're terribly late!' Cecelia called querulously from the parlour.

He pulled a face and Wilhelm laughed and nudged him. 'Your mistress's voice.'

'Coming, *namrata*,' Luca called, 'we were delayed.' He shook the flowers roughly from their wrapping, filled a vase under the tap and shoved them in, flicking them into shape as he left the kitchen.

'I'll give you a hand with this,' Wilhelm said.

He knew his way around the kitchen, fetching more ice and placing a bowl of pâté, crackers and cheese straws on a tray while I poured the drinks. He had long fingernails and he made fussy movements with his hands, shifting plates around unnecessarily. He smelled faintly sweaty and I thought his wispy ponytail could do with a wash; my own recent descent into the world of the grimy had left me sensitized to personal hygiene.

'Are you visiting?' I asked.

'Yes, for a while. I am travelling the world.'

'Where have you been?'

'London is first stop from Rotterdam. It's hard to leave, it's so good here. It's very kind of Cecelia to let me stay in this magnificent place.' He spread a large wedge of pâté on a cracker while he was talking and ate greedily, already helping himself to another. Crumbs fell to the floor and Daphne, who had retreated to her cushion by the cooker, came to investigate. Wilhelm looked down and nudged her away none too gently with his foot.

In the parlour, Luca was sitting by Cecelia, holding her hand while she complained.

'You could have phoned to say that you'd be late. I was worried. What on earth took you so long?' she asked petulantly, tapping his nose forcefully with her forefinger. 'I thought you were just going to the gym and for your singing lesson.'

He ducked his head away from her. 'Sorry, sweetheart. But look at the flowers I brought back for you, for my unique lady.'

She wrinkled her nose, mollified. 'They are so pretty and such a lovely scent! Thank you, darling, you are thoughtful.'

'They're not as pretty or as fragrant as you,' he said gallantly, kissing her cheek.

I had picked up my pad and was sketching as they talked, trying to capture the fluid energy in Luca's stooped posture, the sulky droop of Cecelia's mouth. I looked at her, wondering if she was finding his compliments glib but she was gazing at him fondly.

'Really, Cecelia,' he said, rubbing his forehead wearily, 'the traffic was terrible, it took ages to get to Kensington. Then we met Beatrice, a friend of Wilhelm's, outside Barkers. She's teaching English for the summer in one of those language schools.'

'It's my fault, Cecelia, I delayed him, talking to Beatrice. Poor thing, she arrived from Paris to do this job believing she had been promised accommodation but it was a misunderstanding so she's desperately looking for somewhere to live.' Wilhelm passed round the drinks and offered cheese straws.

'Gosh, this G and T is good!' Cecelia blinked and patted her chest.

Luca laughed. 'Extremely potent, little Marti. You'll never make a profit as a bartender. Only one for you, I think, Cecelia, we don't want you dancing on the tables!'

I didn't look at Luca. I was still annoyed at being called a child and the 'little Marti' name was grating on me. I ate a cheese straw and watched as Wilhelm tucked into his fourth round of crackers and pâté, licking meat from his long fingernails.

'My dancing days are almost over,' Cecelia mused, sipping. Her colour was rising and the tremor in her hands was more pronounced.

'I will dance with you after supper tonight, *amorin*. A waltz, maybe. We will put Strauss on and pretend we are by the Danube, in the moonlight.'

Cecelia chinked her glass against Luca's, spilling a little of the gin. 'I'll drink to that, darling.'

Luca wiped her hand gently with a napkin, smoothing the fingers slowly. 'It might have to be a late supper tonight, I'm afraid. We have to go out for a while again; try and help Beatrice find a place. We left her in a café with the evening papers but you know how quickly rooms go and she isn't earning much. She doesn't know her way around the city, does she, Wilhelm?'

Wilhelm swallowed and coughed. 'No, she hardly knows the place and I wouldn't want her choosing a seedy part. She's a young woman, anything might happen. She already had her purse taken on the tube, the second day she was here.'

Cecelia tutted. 'Dreadful! But how lovely, to find men who are still gallant! It would be terrible if she went to one of those places south of the river where there is so much crime.'

'Exactly.' Luca stood and stretched, his T-shirt riding up over his flat brown stomach. 'But of course, Beatrice won't be able to afford anywhere really decent; we just need to make sure she doesn't end up in one of the worst areas.'

Cecelia put her glass down and pressed her hands to the sides of her head. 'For heaven's sake, what are we thinking of? Beatrice must stay here, with us. There's plenty of room!'

'Are you sure? I wouldn't wish to impose but that would be very kind of you,' Wilhelm said.

'Any friend of Luca's is a friend of mine; one of the family, as it were. It would be a pleasure. Let's arrange it at once. Luca, you can make a bed up – the room near the front door, I think, and we'll get Fortunata to arrange it properly tomorrow. Wilhelm can fetch Beatrice, I shall change and then the four of us can dine together. Fortunata has left pheasant and salad and there are potatoes ready to roast in the oven. And afterwards, we can dance. Luca, your name is on my card!'

He took both her hands and kissed them, nodded to Wilhelm who swiftly vanished. I reluctantly said my good-byes, hoping that Cecelia might ask me to stay for a while longer, even invite me to supper; I was desperate to taste pheasant and watch her waltz with Luca as if they were by the Danube. He might dance with me and I could ask him to drop the 'little Marti' moniker. But Cecelia didn't acknowledge my mumbled farewell. She was following Luca, trying to keep up with him, calling instructions about flannels and towels, flowers for the room, asking should she wear the primrose Dior or the pale-green Jaeger?

Disappointed, I tucked my sketch pad under my arm and wandered down to the garden to see if my toad friend was taking the evening air. The forget-me-not pond was still, as was the garden, no sounds at all. As I was heading back to the basement I saw Wilhelm leave the building and cross the road. He waved to a plump young dark-haired woman who was standing on the pavement and sipping a can of drink, a rucksack beside her. They embraced and kissed. He said something to her and she laughed, making a thumbs up sign. I hurried into Bres's flat; although the atmosphere there was fuggy with smoke, at that moment it somehow seemed fresher than the air in Cecelia's.

6

I was hurrying back along Sloane Street one early evening, my eyes filled with images from the National Gallery. So absorbed had I become in Da Vinci drawings and particularly those of hands and his skill in capturing the folds and textures of cloth, that I'd failed to notice the time slipping away. Bres had asked me to pick up some ice cream on the way home, for supper with the cronies. As I neared Sloane Square I saw Cecelia and Luca on the zebra crossing, his hand under her elbow. She was moving very slowly, as if picking her way through stony terrain and Luca held a palm up forbiddingly to a motorist who had started to edge forwards. When they reached the pavement he steadied her, holding her shoulders. Then he smoothed her hair back from her forehead, kissed her cheek, readjusted her bag which had slipped down her arm and waited while she looked at the summer-dining-themed window display in Peter Jones.

That morning, I had sketched them by the forget-me-not pond; Cecelia on the bench holding Daphne, Luca sitting on the grass, one hand trailing in the water, a songbook on his knee. He was studying Schubert, humming phrases from *Du bist die Ruh*. Cecelia joined in the humming from time to time, saying that she recalled a beautiful concert of Schubert's songs in Vienna. When I finished sketching she pronounced her delight and said that she thought I should become her official artist in residence for the rest of the summer; she would be my temporary patron. Holding her hand out to Luca she asked if this arrangement would meet with his approval. Luca agreed that every artist deserved a benefactor and he would be happy to share her with me for a little while. In fact, he suggested, before I left London an exhibition of my sketches could be held in the drawing-room; a farewell event for me and a demonstration of my talent. I was so impressed, I nearly knocked over the jug of iced lemonade provided by Fortunata as I collected up my pencils. Cecelia had to help me get my balance and she laughed as I apologized, saying not to worry, it was rather good that *she* could be the one doing the steadying for a change.

I looked on as Cecelia pointed to a stack of dishes in the shop window and Luca nodded. Then he opened the door of Peter Jones, standing back with a little bow as Cecelia straightened, smiled up at him and entered. I thought that if I knew nothing about them, if I hadn't heard other people's opinions, I might see them as a lady and her knight, such was the graceful, courteous image they presented. I had noticed several people glancing at Cecelia, then at Luca and I wondered what they were thinking and whether Cecelia was aware of their looks. Luca, as always, gazed around him with an imperturbable expression. He closed the door, obviously not intending to shop with her, looked at his watch and drew out a mobile phone. I watched him talking into it for a few minutes, then he set off at a fast pace, away from me, up the King's Road. I sped on my way in search of a large tub of strawberry-and-vanilla.

I bought the ice cream in the small supermarket across the road from the Fife and Drum where Bres had ordered fish and chips on my first day. The blackboard was outside the door again and I crossed to see what was chalked on it. *Exercise self control; never drink anything stronger than gin before breakfast.* I wondered whether Sylvie Leycroft frequented the bar inside, chatting up the handsome Australian and whether she had maybe inspired the latest maxim.

Those were the days before mobile phones were commonly used, so I was very impressed by Luca's possession of one. People's telephone habits were generally still more circumspect and subject to arrangement. The agreement with my mother was that we would take turns ringing on Thursday evenings. I was aware that I was enjoying myself, sketching in the sun, eating salmon sandwiches, exploring the riches of my surroundings, playing cards with Bres and his cronies and not being at home supporting her. The guilt made me even more angry and unkind. My discomfort when I heard her often tired voice rendered me uncommunicative. It was the people at Dauncey Court who received my smiles and conversation; my love for her was curdled and mean.

She rang that evening, as I was eating ice cream and learning the rules of poker, sharing a hand with Fatso

Flanagan. I dragged myself to the phone. Bres was assuring her that I was fine, living off the fat of the land, on the pig's back.

'Is your grandfather drunk?' she asked as I said hello.

'No. He's had a couple of stouts.'

'What's all that noise, is it a party?'

Castro was singing 'The Gambler' in the background in his deep, growly voice, tapping a percussion with his signet ring on the table: . . . *you've got to know when to hold 'em, know when to fold 'em, know when to walk away and know when to run.* . . .

'Bres's friends are here, playing cards.'

'Righty and that crew?'

'Yes.'

'You're not drinking, are you?'

'No, mother.' I sighed heavily.

'Well . . . that's all right, then. The twins send their love. They miss you. They've drawn some pictures, I put them in the post. We went on the boating lake today so they're tired out, fell asleep as their heads hit the pillows. What have you been up to?'

'Oh, drawing, walking around, going to museums.' That was exactly what I'd told her last time.

'You're not bored?'

'No.'

'Because you can come back if you are, you only have to say.'

'I'm fine.'

'Mr Roberts, the headmaster at Daddy's school, was in touch. He's such a kind man. We discussed a memorial for Daddy and I thought something living would be good, I think that's what he'd have wanted. We talked about a tree in the school grounds. What do you think?'

'Fine, yes.'

Her voice grew thinner. 'Early next year would be the time to plant it. We'd have a little get-together, help put it in. We just have to decide what kind of tree.'

'Ash. That was his favourite.'

'Yes, OK, that's good. I'll tell Mr Roberts, then. I wondered if you'd like to draw a design that we could have put on a little plaque on the tree, with Daddy's name?'

'Mmm, I'll have a think.'

There was a silence, then a whisper. 'I miss him, I miss him so much.'

I chewed at my lip. 'Me too.'

My mother sniffed, blew her nose. 'And Bres, does he say much?'

'Not a lot. He feels the same, though.'

'A man of few words, that Bres.'

'He keeps busy, you know. Says you've got to keep calm and carry on.'

'Oh yes, that was on a World War Two poster he used to have pinned up in the loo when I first knew him.'

'He's got a new painting on the go.'

'Good, OK.' Her voice lifted, a determined effort. 'And have you met anyone interesting who lives there at Dauncey?'

'A couple of people. The gardener's nice, she's called Gina.' I knew I had to offer her something, some flavour of my life but I didn't want to tell her about Cecelia and Luca and particularly about the 'artist in residence' offer. They were my discovery and if I mentioned them she'd start asking questions and then they would be hers as well. She might be sniffy about Cecelia being my patron, there could well be comments about snobs, people born with silver spoons and airs and graces. My mother made claims to socialism and had been a member of the Workers Revolutionary Party for a while when she was doing her nursing training. She was like a dog with a bone when her curiosity was aroused and she had a way of getting things out of me through sheer persistence. I didn't want her interpretation of Cecelia and her world or her opinions and advice on how I should deal with it.

'Sister Tricia sends you all her best.'

'Oh good.'

My mother sighed. 'We might come down to London one day soon, have lunch and you can take us to a museum. The twins would love to see dinosaur skeletons, they've got colouring-books with a story about Diplodocus.' She laughed. 'Gregory says *skellingtons*. Wednesday would be a good day.'

'OK.'

'Right, then, we'll be looking forward to it. I'd best go now, got some ironing to do. Sleep tight, sweet dreams.'

Later, as I was helping Bres clear away ashtrays and glasses, I mentioned the tree memorial idea.

'That would be fitting,' he said softly, running the hot tap, gazing down into the sink. 'In that way, he will outlive us all.'

I remembered what Cecelia had said about desert islands and being marooned. 'You must miss Dad lots,' I ventured.

Bres reached out a wet hand and rested it on the top of my head. 'I've been shook bad, right enough. My heart is torn, pet, my heart is torn. When your grandmother died I was sore-hearted too for many a year, but this is different somehow. It isn't right for your child to die before you; it's as if the sky has fallen.'

'Will you help us plant the tree?'

He raised a washed glass, examined it. 'I will, of course. I could get a sod of turf from home too, so the roots will grow in a wee bit of Ireland.'

'Nobody's thought about you really, have they, Bres?'

He tipped a nail against the glass, making it ring, a clear note. 'Ah now, Marti pet, I'm fairly long in the tooth. When you get to my age you know that if you want to stay in the game, being heart sore is just part of the deal.'

It was that day, I think, that created the real, tangible gulf between myself and my mother and Bres: a gulf of my own making, albeit unwitting. I chose not to tell either of them about my growing friendship with Cecelia and her household and her generosity to me. I desperately wanted something for myself and I certainly wished to avoid their disapproval. I sensed that as soon as you tell another person your thoughts, they earn the right to comment on them; what I had not yet learned was that this is the very balance and check that we use to save ourselves from treacherous reefs.

One afternoon, as I was coming back from the British Museum, I met Cecelia just outside Dauncey Court, holding on to the railings with one hand and her stick with the other, looking at the ground.

'Are you OK?' I asked her, hovering by the steps.

'Yee-es,' she said in her slow way. 'I am concentrating on

breathing. I become a little unsteady at times, quite unexpectedly.'

'Can I do anything?'

'Just wait for a moment, my dear.'

I waited, looking at her bent head and at how thin the spun hair was on her crown, where the skin was dry, parched-looking. The veins on her hands were prominent, raised blue ridges the colour of pale ink. She shuddered, then looked up with her pale, almost translucent eyes.

'What is the saying that people use sometimes when they shiver unexpectedly?'

'I think you mean when a person says that someone has walked over their grave. My grandfather says that, quite often in fact.'

'Does he? He is a kindly man, you must look after him.' She hitched her tiny clutch bag up her arm. 'Would you be very sweet and help me home? I really am rather shaky; silly me, I probably walked too far but I felt so fit when I started out. A case of the spirit being willing and the flesh weak. I believe that I'm eighteen, you see.'

She smiled at me, her sweet smile that lit up her face and made her instantly younger.

'Of course, no problem.'

I walked beside her as she moved slowly. We travelled up in the lift and I told her about my day in the British Museum and how I admired the Celtic silver.

'I do recall seeing some beautiful silver brooches from Verlamion there; they had a kind of spiritual quality – it's hard to describe,' she said. 'By the way, I do hope I'm not inconveniencing you?'

'No, of course not.'

She asked me to fetch her a sherry after she had unlocked the door and gone to her bedroom. There was a decanter in the room, by the French window. She sat and after drinking half a glass of the pale amber wine, her colour improved.

'Ah, that's so much better, I think I became too warm. The sun is quite relentless.'

'You do look brighter. That's a beautiful dress, Cecelia, are those called cap sleeves?'

'Yes, it's a jersey silk, it keeps its shape beautifully. It's a Dior, I bought it in 1970.' She patted the neck, finished her sherry and stood, taking a moment to steady herself. 'Come with me over here and see.'

She was energetic suddenly, animated. She beckoned and I followed her to the wide built-in wardrobe with mirror doors that slid open. It covered half of one wall and was packed with clothes all hung in individual plastic covers. Cecelia gestured at the left-hand section.

'These are all my designer classics. Now, let me see which ones would delight you most.' She teased at the covers with her stick. 'If I point, my dear, can you take a selection out?'

I lifted down the ones she indicated and laid them as instructed on the foot of the bed.

'This cocktail dress,' she said as I unzipped the cover, 'is Balenciaga. I bought it in New York in 1948. It's silk chiffon.'

I ran my fingers lightly over the vivid red poppies with their green stems on black silk. 'When did you last wear this?'

'Oh goodness, that's a question!' She settled both hands

on her stick, pondering. 'I think on the Queen Mary in the early sixties. The pre-dinner cocktails were delicious, I recall. I became very fond of one called London Fog; crème de menthe, anisette and Angostura bitters. Hold it up against you, see how it looks!'

'Are you sure? I don't want to damage it. . . .'

'Nonsense! It would give me pleasure.'

I stepped before the mirror and held it to me, admiring the shaping of the black suede belt and wide flared collar. 'You must have looked stunning,' I said, turning.

Cecelia nodded. 'I had my moments. Now, try on the Dior coat; it was a present to me from my husband for my birthday – 1954, I think, yes.'

I slipped my arms into the yellow tulip-shaped coat and did up the hidden buttons. It had extraordinary contours with its big pockets and three-quarter sleeves. 'You must have caused quite a stir in this, it's pretty unusual.'

'Yes, an eye-turner and such beautiful stitching. You know, I think it's sad that there is so little colour in mass-produced clothing these days; so much drab grey and black everywhere, a kind of lacklustre uniform. However, I must take care not to sound old and cantankerous. Now, do unwrap the Coco Chanel.'

I examined the Chanel, a suit with a knee length skirt and boxy jacket in black jersey wool, with dull gold buttons; simple and classy.

'Look at the hem,' Cecelia instructed. 'It's weighted by a chain to ensure the shape; a Coco trademark. There's that wonderful quote attributed to her: *fashion fades, only style remains the same.* How true – remember that in years to come.'

We unpacked several more; a green chiffon Yves St Laurent evening gown, two Balenciaga sixties-style shift dresses, bright orange and sky blue. Cecelia insisted I hold each one against me before I replaced them in their covers. I loved the feel and cut of the materials, the shaping of skirts and collars as much as the glamour of the design. I was thinking that they would last for ever; I said so to Cecelia and she nodded.

'What a lovely surprise, to have done this,' she said. 'Your figure is so similar to mine when I was young. It brings back special memories to see you with them; reminds me of fun and youth and excitement, of being absolutely one hundred per cent *alive*. My clothes have been very much the story of my life. My husband was a diplomat, you know, and as his wife I had to dress for the occasion, it's all part of flying the flag. My husband genuinely loved to see me in them too, he was one of those rare men who understand shape, line and colour, rather as dear Luca does. I rarely take those particular garments out now, you see, although they still fit, all of them. That does give me satisfaction, I must say.'

She poured herself another sherry as I closed the wardrobe. 'I think I'll have a little nap now.' She yawned. 'What a lovely interlude, though, my dear and so unexpected. Thank you.' She smiled her unmistakable *au revoir* smile.

I drew the cocktail dress as soon as I could that afternoon, capturing the flow and boldness, recalling the smooth warmth of the suede belt. My imagination was full of the sights and textures of the day. I knew what Cecelia meant by that hundred per cent feeling and I was conscious, in a way that I was too young and unformed to name, of her making me aware of it. Now I would call it generosity of spirit.

My bedroom window looked up into a secluded corner of the garden which was mainly in the shade during the day and was dotted with foxgloves and clumps of chives and wild garlic that sent an oniony aroma on the dusk air. There were a number of nights when I was woken by laughter and glasses clinking. I would lie, listening to the faint murmur of voices I knew – Luca's, Wilhelm's, Beatrice's and others unfamiliar to me. The scent of marijuana would mingle with onion, nicotiana and stock. At times there were rustlings, giggles, the sound of running. In the darkness, it sounded like anarchy. In my bed I felt an outsider, the awkward guest hovering on the edges of a room. On some nights I was drawn to the window and peeped out from behind the curtain. Once I saw Wilhelm sitting high in a tree, glass in one hand, long cigarette in the other, and on another occasion he and Beatrice were up there, arms entwined. On one evening there were two men I didn't know, wearing just boxer shorts, one giving the other a piggy back, running in circles until they fell to the grass and embraced.

That evening after my mother's phone call I was wakeful and restless. I heard Luca humming the 'Wedding March' at around 11.30 and a woman's low laugh. I crept to the window. Twitching the curtain, I glanced up and saw him standing between Beatrice and Wilhelm, joining their hands together and faking a blessing. Wilhelm took Beatrice's chin in his hand and kissed her slowly while Luca grabbed petals from a climbing rose and scattered them over their heads. To me it looked like a dream of romance. I let the curtain fall and crept back to bed. I hugged a pillow to my chest, even though it made me hot. It took a long time before sleep caught me in its nets.

The next morning, I walked around that corner of garden, still restless. I didn't know why I was there or what I might be looking for. I stood in the place where I had seen Luca and the others, remembered how Beatrice had placed her fingertips on Wilhelm's shoulders. Beneath a bush I spotted a couple of empty wine and champagne bottles and I removed them so that Gina or Bres wouldn't find them, although whom I was protecting I didn't know.

A few days later I was sprawling in the shade thrown by Pan. In the still air sounds drifted clearly through open windows. Luca's voice came from somewhere above, practising scales and exercises. 'Ta, To, Te, To, Hi, He, Ha, Ho, Hu, Qua, Quo, Que, Quo,' he sang. Then, with growing volume: 'Bring back the boys' big brown blue baseball bats,' and 'Sally saw Sylvester stacking silver saucers side by side.' After the exercises he started rehearsing, pausing and stopping, little runs on the harpsichord, phrases being repeated, the courtly songs I had heard previously; then came a switch to the guitar and Spanish music, rich and fast. Feet suddenly stamped and Wilhelm shouted '*Olé!*' There was laughter and Beatrice squealed: 'Willy, you are a beast!'

For a while I had been lying on my back, tracking wispy clouds across the sky, thinking about my father. After the twins were born, I behaved badly for months, incensed at the invasion of *my* nest. I refused to help with The Calamities' interminable meals, ignored them as much as possible, turned the television up loudly to drown the sound of their squalling and took to stealing small change from my mother's purse and the hallway table, where my father always dropped his. One night, my father slipped a note under my bedroom door.

A few things I cling to in the rough and tumble of life. I call this philosophy THAW: Tolerate others, Hold yourself to honesty, Actively love, Watch your own pettiness.

I read it and cried in shame, because I knew how mean I had been and how much he loved me. Nothing more was said or needed to be said. I tried to mend my ways.

A few months later he took me on a trip to Hadrian's Wall, when the twins were about a year old. Around this period it seemed that my parents divided up their time, with more of my father's being devoted to me. I suspect this may have been a deliberate decision in order to maintain family harmony. We'd driven to Carlisle and walked out in a warm early-morning autumn mist, a picnic in our rucksacks and binoculars at the ready. I had insisted on wearing my new trainers and I developed an agonizing blister on my heel after only a couple of miles. My father collected leaves and deftly made a cool padding for inside my sock as I rested against the base of the wall. *Can you hear those legionaries marching, Marti? Close your eyes and you'll hear them, tramping along, cursing the British weather, wondering if they'll ever get dry again, grumbling about*

THE APPLE OF HER EYE

their pay and rations. I closed my eyes and heard them, felt the rhythm of them on the earth, forgot about my throbbing heel. *Hey, Fergius,* I said in a rough military way, *got anything to chew on this rotten march?* My father rummaged in his pockets. *Here Martillus, fancy a bit of savage Northumbrian mint cake?* The dewy leaves in my sock were soothing, the mint cake warmed my throat and stomach. I had my father, the magician and comforter, all to myself. He hunkered down beside me, chewing on his bar, sunglasses pushed on top of his head. It was a perfect morning, well worth any number of blisters. The mist had cleared, leaving a light blue sky and a cool breeze. There was no one else on the horizon, we had the country as far as the eye could see to ourselves. As we got up to go he ruffled my hair and said what he must have said to me a thousand times: *You're my only Marti in the whole wide world.*

I squeezed my eyes tight, aching for those hours again. There was nothing that anyone could say about his death that would ever console me. Part of my life had gone and was irreplaceable. I knew deep inside that it would always be like that and I would always feel cheated. Other people would miss him terribly and feel their own merciless grief but no one would miss him as I did, because I was the only Marti. After a while I blew my nose and turned to my book. I was engrossed when a shadow teetered across the page.

'Reading anything interesting?' Sylvie Leycroft asked, with a hiccup.

I've always thought that's a particularly dull question as surely no one would read a book they didn't find interesting. If the questioner is enquiring if he or she would find it interesting, how could the reader possibly know?

'Yes,' I said, nodding.

She sat down on the grass beside me with an unexpectedly graceful and fluid sideways swing of her knees. She was wearing a strange combination of scuffed silver ballet pumps, tracksuit bottoms – the kind with elasticated ankles – and a Chinese silk jacket with buttons missing so that a swath of greying bra was revealed. She had a cloth turban around her head with wisps of her salt and pepper hair straying from the edges. The whisky fumes nearly knocked me out as she shifted too close to me.

'I was quite a well-known face at one time,' she informed me in a slurred voice.

'Really?'

'Yes, I was modelling in magazines before I did films. Have you ever seen me in anything?' she demanded, squinting.

I gazed, fascinated at her bulging bosom and fraying bra strap. 'I don't think so.'

'I was in demand in the fifties and sixties. Played with Johnny Mills and Dirk a couple of times. We had such laughs. I used to have cocktails with Diana Dors down Soho.'

'What kind of parts did you play?'

'Gangster's moll, nightclub singer, wisecracking barmaid, naughty nurse. But there's no roles once you hit middle age and my kind of figure went out of fashion – too curvy.' She elbowed me. 'You'll never have that problem.'

I shifted back a bit. 'I expect not.'

'I think women should look like women instead of stick insects. Mind you, my mum used to say that I was well-endowed because I suffered with my glands!'

She found this hilarious. I was worried that I might get another dig in the ribs so I said quickly, 'did you make any films abroad?'

She fiddled in her tracksuit pocket for cigarettes and lighter and lit one, sucking deeply. It reminded me of Gregory and his dummy; there used to be hell to pay if he couldn't find it. My father used to hide spare ones in every room in case of dire emergency. Sylvie drew on it as if it was the last fag on earth. I've never smoked but when I see smokers do that, I get a glimpse of the sheer pleasure they must find in nicotine. She cleared her throat and furrowed her brow in thought, holding her right elbow in her left hand, cigarette at an angle. I watched the smoke hang in the still air.

'I remember we went to Berlin once for a spy thing but only for two days and it rained all the time. I didn't like those German sausages or their beer, far too heavy. There was a chap there, a make-up artist who had the eye for me but I was going out with someone at the time and I was never a two-timer, not like some of the girls I worked with.' She coughed and picked a shred of tobacco from her lower lip. 'Know what my biggest mistake was, though?'

'What?'

'I never made an advantageous marriage. Other actresses, they landed themselves a chap in the business side of films, someone with money and a country residence and vanished to a comfy life. I had romances with actors and always ended up dumped when they moved on.'

'You never married, then?'

'No.' She leaned closer. 'I'll tell you something else I've

never admitted to anyone; no one *ever* asked!' She burst out laughing, startling me. 'No one *ever* asked!' She wiped at her eyes with the hem of her jacket. 'Mind you,' she tapped her nose, 'I didn't do so bad, made some canny investments and bought into this place before property in London went ballistic. Hmm, did I tell you I knew Dirk Bogarde?'

'You mentioned him, yes.'

She fiddled with the buttons of her jacket, pointlessly trying to pull it closed and had just turned to me to speak when there was a crash like glass shattering and raised voices floated on the air from Cecelia's room. The French windows were thrown open, one swinging back on its hinge.

'Don't tell me what to do, this is my home!' Cecelia yelled. There was a surge in her voice, a rawness that I'd never heard.

'Cecelia, calm down, *namrata*. I'm not telling you what to do. I was trying to be helpful.' Luca's tone was tight, with a forced steadiness.

Sylvie and I looked at the balcony as if expecting the two of them to appear front stage. I saw Luca crossing Cecelia's room, hands on hips.

'And don't tell me to calm down!' she shouted. 'I will not be patronized. I've made up my mind and I will send whatever invitations I think fit.'

'OK, Cecelia, go ahead,' Luca said, edgy suddenly. 'But don't come crying to me when your cousin starts interfering in your affairs again. You know he likes to get his foot through the door; remember last time?'

'That was a misunderstanding.'

'Oh, really? That's not what you said afterwards, when you were weeping on my shoulder.'

'I was just upset, I had a headache. It's my birthday, my eightieth birthday. Randolph will be most put out if I don't invite him.'

'Let him be upset,' Luca snapped. 'He's such a fussy old busybody; he'll ruin the evening.'

Cecelia screamed, an ear-splitting shriek. 'Do not speak about him in that way! I will not be dictated to!'

I glimpsed Cecelia's stick waving and Luca putting a hand up to deflect it. My mouth had gone dry and I could feel my heart thumping; I had never before seen people fighting as if they meant it. Sylvie let out a snort and shouted: '*Bravo, encore!*' Luca turned, saw our upturned faces, gave us a filthy look and slammed the French windows shut.

'Damn,' Sylvie said, 'I should have kept shtum. Trouble in paradise, who'd have thought it?' She put a finger to her lips and leaned close to me, whispering. 'She's got a temper, that Cecelia. Darling Luca didn't know that when he took up with her. I could have told him; heard her having a real barney with a taxi driver one day. She doesn't like being crossed, that's what it is, she's not used to it. Her hubby used to give in to her every whim. Mind you, bet Luca's got a fair old temper too, being a Latin. And he knows which side his bread's buttered; I hear she's having completely refurbished rooms done for him with his own ensuite and whirlpool bath, one of those ones set into the floor. Thousands, it's costing her, but no expense is spared where Luca is concerned. That harpsichord she got him last Christmas is worth a king's ransom, never mind all the singing lessons she pays for.'

'Did you know Cecelia's husband, then?'

'Oh yes, I knew the gorgeous Bartholomew; Olly, as he was known. I met them once, years ago, at a party at the Austrian Embassy. Quite the golden couple they were. You could see he reckoned the sun shone out of her proverbial. The other thing Luca doesn't know is that Randolph was very thick with the two of them, used to join them abroad for holidays. In fact, I think Randolph fancied Olly although I wouldn't imagine the affection was mutual, Olly played a straight bat.' She flicked her cigarette end into the bushes and rubbed her thighs, groaning. 'My legs aren't behaving too well today, sweetie. Could you possibly run to the shops for me on your supple young pins, get me a bottle of wine?'

I had to look away from the sheer need on her face. 'I'm sorry, I can't. I'm under age.'

She pulled a sour face. 'Bloody nanny state. Bloody interfering Nosy Parkers. When I was your age I was always nipping down the local for my nan.'

I shrugged, looked regretful.

'Sod it then, if you want a job done, you have to do it yourself. I'll have to get a taxi.'

I watched her weave across the garden, stopping to smell a flower. She turned and waved to me.

'Remember to take time to smell the roses!' she called.

I waved back, resisting an impulse to go with her; I couldn't because in half an hour I was due to meet Cecelia and accompany her to her dressmaker.

7

We drove by car to South Kensington, but not in an ordinary cab; it was a Bentley from a firm that Cecelia used regularly and had an account with. Bres called it Toff's Taxis and advised me to inhale the smell of leather. Cecelia was all in white: a belted dress and jacket, peep-toe sandals and clutch bag. She looked crisp on a hot day and perfectly calm, no sign of her earlier argument with Luca. As we drove she told me that Ivan Karastov, her dressmaker, was a genius and a gem; he had been making her dresses for over forty years. I asked if he was Russian and Cecelia said yes, that he grew up in Leningrad and had known Rudolf Nureyev because he worked in the wardrobe department of the Kirov. I sat back in the vast, cushiony seat and gazed through the tinted windows; the streets and people drifted by as the quietly purring car glided along. These were the roads I had walked, observing cleaning women and nannies, witnessing my naked man, stopping to smell a hedge, smiling at a porter as he stood with his arms held behind his back. In the Bentley we were so sealed away from the world outside, it was like observing a silent film. I thought about how different it was to be rich and protected constantly from the rest of humanity.

Ivan Karastov was a plump, gnomelike figure dwelling in a dark, fusty flat just behind South Kensington station; every three minutes or so there was the faint rumble of a train, like a giant growling below. He had a womanly shape with well-padded hips that stretched his trousers. His face and hands were pale, the skin doughy and he blinked a great deal. I wondered if this was because he stayed in most of the time, labouring over seams and tucks. Cecelia called him Count and he addressed his customer as Madame B. His living-room was lined with bookcases on two walls and on the other two hung large, foreboding paintings of forests with gnarled trees. The carpet was worn and covered in strands of thread and his sewing machine stood in the window bay, a treadle type with a tall stack of glossy fashion magazines beside it.

The dress was being made for Cecelia's approaching birthday. It was standing on a dummy in the centre of his small living-room, eau-de-Nil satin with a flattering boat neck, ankle-length, straight and with a slight flare at the hips. It was almost finished, beyond the fitting stage, which disappointed me as I wanted to see Cecelia in it. Instead, there was talk of final adjustments, accessories and shoes while the count fussed with a gilt spherical urn that sat on three legs on a side table, rattling and gasping. When he turned a tap at the bottom a stream of boiling water rushed into a jug. He saw me gazing and beckoned me over.

'Do you like my samovar?'

'I've never seen one before, it's amazing.'

'It is an old Russian way of boiling water, usually for tea

but I make my coffee with it at this time of the afternoon. This was my grandmother's and the sound of it comforts me, takes me back to her house. Be careful, it's very hot. We used to gather in the late afternoons, all of us, and spend an hour drinking tea and talking.'

He was only a little taller than me and his breath smelled like nail varnish, not unpleasant but strong. I looked at the back of the samovar but saw no electric lead. 'What heats the water?'

'You can get electric ones now but I use charcoal. My grandmother used to use wood or pine cones. In Russia there is an expression: "to sit by the samovar", which means to have a leisurely chat and drink copious quantities of tea. My grandmother took hers with lemon.'

When he gave us the coffee it was in tiny cups, a sweet, dark brew; with it we had thin arrowroot biscuits.

'Have you ever thought of being a model?' Ivan asked me.

'Me? No, I think I want to be an illustrator or designer; an architect maybe.' I was flattered, though, at the implied compliment.

'Shame. She has the figure, don't you think?' he said to Cecelia. Biscuit crumbs flaked on his chest and he flicked them away on to the dusty carpet.

'Yes. As long as she achieves the height. She would have to develop style, of course, she's rather fond of jeans and T-shirts. But you know, these days, young women are very serious. There doesn't seem to be much time for fun and glamour, Count.'

'Are you really a count?' I asked as I sipped the scalding coffee.

'Yes, but it is not a title I use. It belongs to another time and place. Madame kindly addresses me by it.'

He nodded at Cecelia who smiled back, holding her coffee cup beneath her nose.

'Now, you are coming to my party, Count?'

'I will be honoured. This young lady will be there?'

I was embarrassed because Cecelia hadn't invited me, but she didn't miss a beat; she put her cup down and said of course, and that I would be a very special guest, being the youngest as well as her artist in residence.

Back in the Bentley Cecelia hummed and smiled.

'I feel so much better after seeing the Count. He is a constant light glowing in a changing world, always there with his samovar and biscuits. No matter how long I was out of the country, however far away we had roamed, nothing had ever altered, nothing had ever been moved, not even an inch, the next time I saw him. I expect he had enough radical upheavals in his early days to last him a lifetime. He had almost nothing, you see, when he came to London, except his samovar. He was clutching it when Olly and I met him at Heathrow. He managed to slip away while the Kirov was in Rome, just a year or so before Nureyev defected.'

I had a vision of the count running down the steps of a plane into freedom, coat-tails flapping, his arms cradling his grandmother's samovar.

'It's like a novel or a film, it's so romantic,' I said.

'Only from a distance. In real life there isn't much romance in having to leave all your family and friends behind you.'

'I did like his flat. It's a cosy burrow.'

Cecelia tapped my arm. 'He does have something of the hobbit about him, it's true. Darling, would you indulge me while I stop at my jeweller's? I want to buy something to go with my dress and I have ordered a surprise for Luca.' She called to the driver, 'Sloane Street, please.'

We were the only customers in the jeweller's, which was cool and quiet. Leather chairs were pulled up for us and a man in a pinstripe suit appeared who looked like the manager. He obviously knew Cecelia, said how nice it was to see her again and asked after her health. She nodded in what I now recognized as her brisk manner when she couldn't be bothered with someone and took a strip of the dress fabric from her bag. She stated that she wished to purchase a set of earrings and necklace to complement her gown.

'Silver, I rather think,' she said, 'and delicate, no fuss.'

I loved Cecelia's language, the way she said purchase instead of buy, complement rather than go with. I glanced in a case of rings beside me and noted that there were no prices. Bres maintained that if something didn't have a price attached, he couldn't afford it. The manager murmured and swiftly fetched several trays of items and a mirror which he placed in front of Cecelia. She took her glasses out and examined the jewellery, placing the fabric over one shoulder while she gazed at her reflection. The air conditioning in the shop was so high I shivered but Cecelia didn't notice, intent on her purchase. At last she nodded, choosing a fine, two-strand necklace in a star pattern with tiny earrings to match. She also wished to collect the cufflinks she had ordered last month.

'And now,' she said, turning to me and tapping my arm with her forefinger, 'I wish to purchase you something to thank you for sketching me with my scent bottles – or one of them, whichever one seems right for the occasion.'

'But I haven't done it yet.'

'You are a very literal young woman! Well then, you must do the deed soon. In the meantime, as we are here and as you have accepted an honorary position in my household, we should strike while the iron is hot. What kind of jewellery do you like?'

I was nonplussed. 'I don't know, I've never really worn any. . . .'

'Then that has to be remedied. Every woman should be partnered by jewels that translate her to the world and you are on the brink of womanhood. Let me think.'

She snapped her glasses off and twirled them while the manager stood waiting.

'A ring, definitely: a quiet statement. When is your birthday?'

'February the fourth.'

'Then you must have your birthstone, an amethyst. Bring some, please, for slender fingers.'

Another tray was brought of amethyst rings, from the deepest purple to pale lilac. I looked at them, nestling in their blue-velvet bed and immediately knew the one I wanted, the palest oval lavender blush set in a fine silver frame. When I tried it on the middle finger of my left hand it fitted perfectly.

Cecelia lifted my hand approvingly. Her hand was cold, her touch as light as a leaf. 'A good choice, Martina.' She looked at me thoughtfully, her gaze soft and unfathomable.

'The amethyst is a stone offering peace and protection. That is a gift I would very much like to give you, you deserve it and need it.'

I blinked and focused on my finger. The stone did look kindly, its paleness suggesting tranquillity. The manager clicked his fingers for the jewellery to be wrapped but I said I would like to wear mine. He opened a black leather box and showed Cecelia the cufflinks, confirming that they were mother of pearl and black onyx. She touched them lightly, nodding. I asked her what her birthstone was.

'Peridot, darling. It's a beautiful lime green. I have a bracelet made of it.'

'And what does it offer?'

'Its special quality is protection against evil.'

I watched as Cecelia unscrewed a sleek fountain pen and wrote a cheque for just under £3,000 in her unsteady hand. She wore a variety of jewels during the brief time I knew her but I never saw her with the peridot bracelet; I couldn't help thinking afterwards that she might well have benefited from its safeguarding attributes.

In the lift at Dauncey Court Cecelia told me not to mention Luca's present; it was a surprise, one that she wanted to give him on her birthday, so that he could wear them to the party. Luca opened the door for Cecelia as soon as we got out of the lift, and came forward to bend and kiss her. He smelled strongly of a spicy scent and his hair was damp, as if he had just showered.

She put her hands up and held his face. 'Mmm, you do smell good after the dust of the city.'

He cradled her elbows lightly. 'Oh, *amorin*, you look

tired,' he crooned. 'You are over time for your tablets, you know; it's naughty of you to stay out so long.' He gave me an accusing look as if I was responsible. 'Come, I have made you tea and tiny bruschetta, just as you like them with a little tomato and basil.' *Bayzil*, he pronounced it, and *tomayto*, the American way.

Cecelia did suddenly look tired and pale, more stooped.

'I'll be off then,' I said. 'Thank you so much for my gift, Cecelia, it's very kind of you and I love it.'

'Oh, have some tea,' she invited, 'and we can discuss tomorrow.'

Luca had started to lead her into the flat but he stopped in his tracks. 'Gift?' he asked, turning, nose raised. I was minded of an animal, scenting danger or another predator.

'Yes, I purchased a delightful ring for our new friend. Let's get inside, I do need to sit down and remove these shoes which are beautiful but less than comfortable.'

We processed slowly to the drawing-room. As we passed the bedroom where Beatrice was staying I heard a hairdryer whining and the thud of bass guitar; Mick Jagger was singing about a honky tonk woman and Wilhelm's voice joined in as the chorus started. There were four men in overalls working in the knocked-through room, which, I had learned, was to be Luca's music study.

'Have you decided on the shelving you want yet, darling boy?' Cecelia asked Luca.

'I am still looking. I think walnut, perhaps. The Jacuzzi and bidet will be delivered on Monday, by the way.'

'When will it all be finished?'

'In a fortnight. The soundproofing in the study is excellent, I must say. I tested it yesterday.'

In the drawing-room Luca knelt and removed Cecelia's shoes and brought her tablets from her pillbox.

'I don't need the pink one, do I?' she asked vaguely, yawning.

'You forgot it at lunchtime, *namrata*. Best to make it up now, otherwise you know your hands get shaky.'

She popped them in her mouth. 'How well you look after me.' She sighed.

'Here, we know what you need, don't we?' Luca pulled up a stool and sat down, took her right foot on his knee and started to massage it, both hands working, agitating each of her toes separately.

I looked at one of the paintings, feeling awkward. It was by Frederick Leighton, a small study of a smiling Greek girl that I thought coy and fussy. I had decided then that most Victorian artists didn't much impress me, unlike Victorian architects. The painting didn't seem to match the creator of Leighton House, which I had visited and found satisfyingly beautiful and austere; I was too young to have discovered that most people carry within them conflicting aspirations and talents.

'Now, there we are. All better?' Luca had finished Cecelia's left foot and rose from the stool, lifting both her feet on to it.

'Much,' Cecelia said drowsily.

'Little Marti can help me bring in the tray while you put your feet up.'

'Thank you, darling. I am rather bushed, it's been a busy day but we got a lot done, several things ticked off my list. The dress is beautiful, you will be thrilled when you see it. We must send the invitations soon, in the next couple of days.'

'Of course. Close your eyes for a few moments. What was it Olly used to say?'

Cecelia smiled and looked misty. 'I must examine the insides of my eyelids.'

Luca beckoned me and I followed him to the kitchen. The Chieftains were playing now in Beatrice's room, a melody that I recognized, 'The Foggy Dew'.

'Are *amorin* and *namrata* Maltese words?' I asked Luca as he switched on the kettle. There were lovely aromas of garlic and herbs; I was aware of my stomach grumbling and wished that I had less of a Pavlovian reaction whenever food was around.

He stuck his hands in his jeans pockets and rested against the counter, crossing his ankles. He was dressed all in black, his shirtsleeves rolled to the elbows. His dark eyes were steady. 'That's right.'

'What do they mean?'

'They mean *love bird* and *sweetheart*. They are commonly used terms of affection.'

He looked straight at me. I was twisting the ring on my finger, unused to its being there.

'Is that your gift?' he asked, stepping forward.

I raised my hand, held it out for him to see. 'Yes, it's my birthstone. It's lovely.'

He took my hand for a moment, tilting it from side to side, and I knew that I had wanted him to. I felt a flush on the back of my neck.

'Very nice, pretty,' he said, letting go and opening the fridge. He looked in, studying the contents as if he could learn something from them. 'Cecelia is fond of you, that's for certain. I think she sees some of herself in you, as a young girl.' He took out a carton of milk, held it for a moment, his back to me, then moved over to the kettle as it boiled and clicked. 'The argument we had earlier, it was nothing, you know. I'm sure Sylvie Leycroft was making the most of it. You mustn't take any notice of her, she's a stupid woman and an alcoholic. Cecelia and I are close friends and we both have intense, artistic temperaments so occasionally we get cross with each other. This is what happens between people, you understand?' He glanced at me, kettle poised mid-air.

I didn't understand but I nodded because it sounded adult, complex and wise.

'Good,' he said. 'It's good, little Marti, that you are an intelligent, talented girl. Yes, I think that is the case and I think that these bruschetta will also be good.'

Beatrice wandered in, flip-flops slapping, wearing a silky dressing gown, brushing back her heavy hair. Collecting the debris from the brush with swift movements, she twirled it between her fingers and let it drift to the floor where it sat like a little nest. She noticed me watching and smiled.

'Fortunata will clear it,' she said in her tight, thin voice. 'That treasure lives to clean!' She clicked her fingers, singing, *'When the sun fills the sky like a big pizza pie, that's amore!'* She sniffed at the bruschetta, laid on a plate with sprigs of basil laced around the rim. 'Mmm, heavenly, they look so tasty!'

She went to take one from the plate, treading heavily but Luca tapped her hand away.

'Not for you, not today. You can get your own food,' he said coolly, looking her up and down. 'Or maybe even better, go on a diet.'

She pulled a face, drawing the up the neck of her gown, chewing on a stubby fingernail. 'Mean old Luca, you are nasty sometimes, I think.' She looked at me. 'Don't you think he's mean?'

I shrugged. 'He hasn't been mean to me.'

Luca laughed and brought me the plate. 'You have a careful turn of phrase, little Marti, I like that and I like your clear grey eyes.'

He blew a wisp of hair from my forehead as he handed over the bruschetta, his warm breath tickling my skin, making my stomach knot in a way that I found alarming and beguiling. I looked at him and it was as if a key turned suddenly and unexpectedly inside me, unlocking and locking at the same moment.

Maybe it was inevitable that I would fall for Luca: just a matter of time. After that evening he started to occupy my thoughts more and more. He literally went to my head, unexpectedly taking up residence; oddly enough he became my own very personal artist in residence. He was my first crush and perhaps he was my first love. I was unformed, impressionable and teeming with stealthy hormones as well as profound sadness; deep down I was lonesome and ready to be overwhelmed, just as Cecelia had no doubt been some years previously. I would think that Luca always, before and after Dauncey days, homed in on women who were vulnerable with an unerring radar. He was in all ways a large character with his deep, authoritative voice, his physicality and charisma, his air of command. I had heard the dishonesty in his tone when he spoke to Cecelia but I quelled my doubts about him. I knew very little of how the world worked and I was too immature and fanciful to weigh up the evidence before me. Confidence and presence are powerful male qualities to many women and particularly to a receptive teenager. I was drawn to him and the idea of him. I dwelled on his remarks to me, tracking back through all our contacts and meetings, turning them over and over, extracting every ounce of meaning; he thought I was intelligent and talented, he liked my grey eyes and the way I spoke. He admired my drawings, implied that we understood each other. I was discovering the addiction of attraction and like any addict, I sought the source of my craving.

I was no longer annoyed by *little Marti*; suddenly it was a term of true endearment and I longed to hear him call me that. I hung around the garden, hoping to see him and lingered in the hallways in the mornings, chatting to Elena. I had no idea of the pattern of his days, or even if there was one, so I had to live in anticipation of a sighting; I knew that he went to the gym and had singing lessons but the details of his movements eluded me. I had the excuse of my sketching, but too often when I rang the bell of the flat I found Cecelia alone and I ended up drawing her or the impatient Daphne. Occasionally I heard him singing and took my sketchpad beneath the open windows so that I could fill my imagination with his scales and lyrics. Never had the lute sounded so plaintive and mysterious. When there were songs I knew, 'La Mer', 'Nature Boy', I sang along softly in accompaniment. My daydreams were frequently of the naïvely sentimental variety; I imagined that Cecelia offered to send me to an exclusive, private school in Kensington where my talent could blossom and that Luca, already secretly in love with me, would wait until I was older before declaring himself. I blush to think of the wedding I pictured, an ancient, ghostlike Cecelia in the wings, graciously conceding, giving her blessing to the joyful couple, allowing the young people to have their happiness.

Of course, all this pubescent fervour predated the events at her birthday party which shattered my far-fetched notions and sowed the seeds of rancour.

Once a month Cecelia held a soirée. These had been instigated after Luca's arrival and were mainly a showcase for his talents. In the winter a huge log fire was laid in the drawing-room, and in summer air-conditioning units were brought in. Food was ordered from a caterer called Connoisseur Cuisine; canapés, dim sum, savoury and sweet pastries, washed down with Krug champagne and fine wines. These refreshments were served by the catering staff in black uniforms who circled silently, ready to replenish glasses and offer another tasty bite to the hungry. The guests were members of local musical and choral groups, people from radio, including the BBC and anyone else who Luca or Cecelia thought might assist in furthering his artistic career.

Gina had told me about the soirées, using these as another example of Luca's freeloading and Cecelia's credulity. I was thrilled when my loitering in the foyer paid dividends one afternoon. Luca passed through, talking to the caterer on his mobile, saying that a vegan was attending; could they make sure there were some excellent offerings as this was an important person. He smiled at me, melting my bones and asked me what I was up to. I stammered that I was examining the mouldings in the cornices, the shapes were fascinating.

'You're a funny little Marti,' he said. 'It must get a bit tedious for you here sometimes. I love my Nannu but I wouldn't want to stay with him for too long.' He clicked his fingers. 'Come to our soirée tonight; you'll enjoy yourself and it would be good to have you there. Anyway, as our artist in residence you should be there. You can sketch me – one artist capturing another; 7 p.m. sharp.'

I was warm with delight. 'Should I dress up?'

'Smart casual,' he said, taking the stairs at a run. 'See you later.'

I spent the rest of the day feeling as if I had a temperature. I couldn't settle to anything. In the end I went for a long walk along the Thames path as far as Chelsea Harbour. As I rambled I replayed his words over and over; he had said it would be good to have me at the soirée and had requested a drawing, identifying our shared artistic gifts. His smile had been sunny, he had been concerned about how I was feeling. My step was buoyant. I watched the boats, dredgers and river cruisers, the trains crossing near Battersea Bridge, the planes that banked low, flying straight down the path of the Thames towards Heathrow. I hummed the song, 'Trains and Boats and Planes' and considered what to wear. On the King's Road I called into a chain store and asked a young woman assistant what would count as 'smart casual'. Just something simple,' she said, 'plain trousers and a shirt or blouse.' I had dark-grey jeans with me, so I looked at the racks of tops and, remembering Cecelia's comment about lack of colour in clothes, I bought a turquoise cotton shirt with a mandarin collar and a necklace of tiny turquoise and grey beads in the accessories section. I felt a strange thrill as the assistant wrapped the necklace in tissue paper.

Bres was at Newmarket for the day, not due back until late, so I left him a note and checked myself one more time in the mirror at five to seven. I seemed to look both smart and casual, my hair parted on the side, the shirt fitting neatly on my waist. My grey eyes, which Luca liked, were enhanced by the necklace. I had spent so long in a steaming bath that my cheeks were flushed. I hoped it would look more like a glow when I got to Cecelia's.

Fortunata opened the door to me. I had forgotten how small and slight she was, inches shorter than me. She was wearing a black dress with a full-length white apron and she bowed slightly as she showed me in, pressing her hands together. There were already a dozen people in the drawing-room. Nat King Cole was singing about Moon River in the background. I looked for Luca and saw him standing by the harpsichord, talking to a tall man, equal in height to him who was balancing a vol-au-vent in one hand and a wine-glass in the other and was still managing to look elegant. Luca was wearing a scarlet silk scarf at the neck, inside a black shirt. I thought he could be a pirate who had just sailed up the Thames. A waitress stopped by me and offered a tray, asking what my preferred drink was? I took two tiny spring rolls and said I would like an apple juice. She said of course and vanished to get it, smiling. I had a fleeting mental image of my mother struggling with the Calamities and erased it as quickly as it had appeared. I ate the spring rolls in two fragrant bites and crossed the room to where Cecelia was sitting, talking to Beatrice and another woman.

'Martina, how lovely that you could come,' Cecelia said, as if I might have had to turn down several other possible social engagements that evening. 'Luca said he had invited you and I am thrilled that you will capture us with your skill of hand and eye. This is Leandra, a friend of Beatrice's. She is from Bournemouth.'

'We work together, teaching languages,' Leandra said. 'Luca has told me about you. I love your necklace.'

She had shiny skin, a quick smile and rapid style of talking. I watched her lips as she spoke of how much she loved London, how she had known the minute she met Beatrice that they were going to be the best of friends, how many of her students were hopeless and had no idea that you must study in your spare time. I was interested only in the fact that Luca had been speaking about me. What had he been saying – that I was talented, interesting, pretty?

'How long have you known Luca?' I asked when she drew breath.

'Oh, we met just the other day – Beatrice and I were having coffee when he passed by.'

'Leandra lived in Geneva for some time, we were discussing places we knew,' Cecelia told me.

The waitress appeared with my apple juice and another tray of food. We all chose our mouthfuls. Beatrice knocked her drink, spilling some but made no move to wipe the side table it was standing on. She was wearing a black low-cut top and dabbed crumbs of food from her cleavage with her chewed fingertip, popping them in her mouth. I listened to Cecelia and Leandra discuss the lakes and skiing while I sought out Luca. There he was, coming towards us, a glass in his hand.

'Hello, fair ladies! And little Marti, my favourite artist, you made it. I am about to perform.' He bent down to Cecelia. 'I have been in long discussions with Piers Leith, he is very interested and has asked me to audition for him.'

That must be the important vegan, I thought.

'Oh, darling Luca!' Cecelia said, taking his hand, 'that really is marvellous!'

He placed a kiss on the back of her fingers. 'Now I must sing for my supper,' he declared, taking a sip from his glass. 'Will you do the honours, Cecelia?'

She took his arm and they walked slowly to the harpsichord. The room had filled with people who were drinking, nibbling and talking. There was a tremendous energy and vibrancy. Wilhelm was chatting to a couple of women, supping beer from a bottle. He was the smartest I'd ever seen him, in dark-brown cotton trousers and a cream shirt with sleeves rolled up. Cecelia smiled around as she made her progress, her head high. Luca sat and Cecelia stood beside him. He played a chord, Cecelia clapped her hands and the room, which was now full, was silent, waitresses stopping in their tracks.

'Welcome to you all,' Cecelia said. 'We have come to love these gatherings and I do hope that you are all having a wonderful time. Now, I would like to introduce to you Mr Luca Gonzi, who will play and sing a selection of music for harpsichord, lute and guitar.'

After applause, Cecelia took a seat to one side of Luca. He worked his way through a repertoire of medieval and modern music. I inched my way along the side of the room, clutching my apple juice, my throat too choked to swallow. I found an empty chair behind Piers Leith, and drew it to one side so that I had a good view of Luca. I was gratified to hear Piers clap loudly when Luca sang the madrigal about the nightingale, the one I had heard him play the first day I met him in the garden. The room was warm despite the air conditioning. I sketched quickly, as if my life depended on it, my pencil dancing on the paper. I felt as light as air and rosy with yearning as Luca announced that his final song was dedicated to his dear friend and patron, Cecelia. Taking his guitar, he walked to the window and stood so that the evening sun shone behind him, glancing fierily on his scarlet scarf. It seemed to me that he glowed like an angel. This was a Maltese folk song, he told us, from the Ghana tradition and it spoke of hospitality and kindness to the stranger. He sang quietly in Maltese, his voice mellow and mild. It was an Arabic sounding tune, plangent. His eyes met mine for a long moment as he repeated what sounded like a chorus. Warm as I was, I had goose bumps on my arms. My pencil was slippery between my fingers. Cecelia led the loud applause when he finished. I sidled away as the guests left, craving solitude and time to think over that glance. He had dedicated the song to Cecelia but I was the one he had looked at. I was glad that Bres was still not back. I crept into bed and closed my eyes, reliving every moment of the evening.

8

Puberty must be the most secretive, guarded time in life. Teenagers are like spies, surveying a mysterious world, emotions lurking under cover, trying to break the codes that allow access to adult know-how. I woke up one morning and as I opened my eyes the thought flowered that I must follow Luca for a day. I turned it over, a delicious anxiety in the pit of my stomach. Why wait when I could act? The idea of being near to him yet unseen was enthralling; the mixture of risk and closeness, of proxy intimacy, of observation, being a hidden participant of his reality, was too much of a lure for reflection.

I packed my light rucksack with sketching equipment, a cheese sandwich, apple, banana and cartons of orange juice, telling Bres that I was off to the V&A and wouldn't be back till evening. He was deep in concentration, studying the form at Newmarket and gave me a thumbs-up. By 9 a.m. I had positioned myself across the road from Dauncey Court, at the side of the flats housing the woman who groomed herself on her balcony. I had no idea how long I might have to wait. After half an hour had ticked by it occurred to me that Luca might be staying in, to rehearse or supervise renovations or sit with Cecelia doing tapestry work. So taken had I been with my idea and the adrenalin rush of making it real, this possibility had not dawned on me. I bit into an apple, determined to wait as long as it took, enjoying the fever of anticipation in my veins. There was an overcast sky and a cooling breeze but I was warm with fervour.

He emerged after another half-hour, a guitar over one shoulder, a small square package under the other arm. He wore jeans with a purple linen jacket and stopped to retie a shoelace and adjust his sunglasses before running lightly down the steps and setting off towards Victoria. I followed, keeping well behind. If he should see me I would tell him that I was going to a museum. I had already practised my script before the bathroom mirror, the nonchalance with which I would inform him. He set a fast pace and I had a stitch before we reached Buckingham Palace Road. He turned down a side street and entered a shop that had a window displaying a grand piano covered in sheet music. I was glad to stand inside a bus shelter across the road, watching through the window as Luca took the guitar from its case and showed it to a woman who nodded, turning it this way and that before writing in a book on the counter. I guessed that some kind of repair was being discussed. Watching his shoulders move, his expressive hands and handsome profile, I was dizzy with adoration.

I ducked down as he left the shop, now carrying the square parcel in front of him, cradling it like a baby. He looked at his watch and turned back to Buckingham Palace Road where the traffic was insistent, fast. My stitch gone, I resumed my tracking. I found that I was smiling with purpose and exhilaration. Some time in a distant future, I imagined, I might tell him about the day I was a secret agent on his trail; he would tease me in that drawling tone he used, trace his fingers lightly on my hand. He cut expertly through leafy side streets heading in the direction of Knightsbridge. Once he stopped and took his mobile phone from his pocket, looking around as he spoke. I thought he might be about to turn and my mouth dried. I pressed against a tree trunk, feeling the rough bark against my face. Off he went again, nodding to a man who was walking half a dozen dogs on leashes.

Nearing Sloane Street, he strode up steps and through swing doors of a tall building with vans parked outside. They were being loaded and unloaded; crates, boxes, chests of drawers, sideboards and rolls of carpet came and went. Gilt letters arched over the doors informed me that the business was Newley & Fromhold: Valuers, Restorers and Auctioneers. I watched as a tallboy and huge mirror were manoeuvred from a van and carried to a door further along the street where a man in a light-brown dustcoat ticked items off on a list.

I waited for nearly forty minutes, walking up and down, watching the activity on the pavement, the straining, shifting, brow-mopping. I sipped at a carton of juice, then crossed the road to a chemist's that called itself an apothecary and tried out some perfume-testers and moisturizers. I was back on the pavement, highly scented, when Luca reappeared without his parcel. His burdens gone, he stuck his hands in his pockets and walked more slowly, almost at a sauntering pace, to Chelsea Green where he waved to a

group of people sitting at a table outside a restaurant. I
hovered in the doorway of a cake shop. I could see Wilhelm
sitting with legs sprawled but I didn't know the other men
and women. There were a few minutes of air kisses, shoulder taps and handshakes, then Luca sat and poured wine
from a bottle sitting in an ice bucket. I could tell by the
sepia-covered awning, the heavy tablecloths and wine
arrangements and the formal attire of the waiter who
quickly appeared that it was an expensive eatery, even for
this affluent part of the capital.

The sky had cleared, the breeze was quietening. The
restaurant was on the sunny side of the street, the table
sheltered by the awning. Menus were perused, discussions
held. There was much laughter. More wine appeared,
followed by trays of food. I saw asparagus, baskets of bread
rolls, pâté, some bowls of soup. My stomach rumbled; it
was almost one o'clock. I also needed a toilet. I reckoned
that this was not going to be a quick lunch. I looked around;
there was a small café nearby and I had ten pounds in my
purse.

I ordered a milk shake, the cheapest item on the menu,
used the ladies and then sat on a high stool at a counter
that looked directly across to the restaurant. I placed my
rucksack on my lap, sneaked pieces of my cheese sandwich
from its wrapping and palmed them into my mouth.
Shaded and secret, I took out my sketch pad when I had
finished eating and drew a rapid picture of Luca and his
friends. The light spilled around them. Waiters removed
plates, brought more, ferried wine. The laughter grew
louder. A tall blonde woman stood, lurching slightly, and
took a photograph as they all leaned inward, some putting

arms around shoulders. Luca smiled up at her, raising his glass. Then she crashed back into her chair, her arms flying up. I stopped drawing and stared; were any of these women interested in Luca? He was sitting between Wilhelm and another man, his chair slightly pulled back. I couldn't see that he was focusing on anyone in particular. I took a sip of milk shake, rolled the cool glass against my forehead. After drying my damp fingers on a napkin I took my pencil again. I had caught the line of Luca's chin well and the drape of his jacket on his chair. I shaded his jawline, my pencil lingering on the curl of hair behind his ear.

At three o'clock the group had desserts and coffee. I bought another milk shake and a muffin and spun them out. When the bill arrived across the road, Luca reached into his wallet and paid with a credit card. He handed Wilhelm some notes and rose, the first to leave. I gathered up my things and sidled out. Luca held his jacket over his shoulder, making another call on his mobile phone as he walked. Near Sloane Square he entered a barber's where he spent an hour having his hair washed and trimmed, then a head massage and a shave. I examined expensive pens and leather luggage in between peeping through the window to monitor his progress and watched American tourists stagger past with heavy carrier bags.

Then it was back to Dauncey Court, Luca hurrying, glancing at his watch. I thought he might be worrying that Cecelia would complain about his long absence. I slowed my own pace, no longer needing to keep up. I stopped by the blackboard at the Fife and Drum to read the latest maxim. *You've got to believe in something. I believe I'll have another drink.*

In the basement at Dauncey Bres was replacing light bulbs, standing on a stepladder.

'You look tired, pet,' he said. 'Don't be wearing yourself out at those museums, you need energy for growing. Will we have cheese and tomato omelettes for tea?'

I helped him beat eggs and grate cheese while he talked about Mr Courteney being given notice to quit and the trouble the managing agents were having with his solicitor. I nodded, barely hearing him, lost in an exhausted Luca reverie.

When my mother phoned to report that the twins had come down with mumps and the proposed London trip was cancelled, I felt traitorously pleased.

'You mustn't come anywhere near us or vice versa,' she said, delivering unwitting music to my ears, 'because you haven't had it and believe me, you don't want it at your age, it would be very painful.'

'Are they all swollen up?' I asked.

'Yes, like little toads. Ursula calls it 'the monks'. Isn't that funny?'

'Mmm, certainly is. So, how long does it last?'

'Up to a fortnight or more. We'll have to rearrange our museum trip for later in the summer.' Her voice suddenly thinned. 'I suppose because they're ill, they've both been pining for Daddy. Asking after him a lot. Sister Tricia suggested that I put together a book for them about him, with stories and photographs. You know, the times he spent with them, the things they did. Our family, Martina, as it used to be.'

My mother only called me Martina when she was cross

or upset. At that moment, it was an appeal to Martina as an almost adult, someone who might reach out and offer some comfort. Except, of course, that Martina was still too ice-covered, self-interested and hazy with hormones to respond; you don't get much warmth when you reach into the freezer and I was as capable of giving her consolation as a packet of frozen peas.

'Yeah,' I muttered. 'I know.'

My mother breathed in. 'Well, anyway; do you think the book thing's a good idea?'

'Absolutely. Brilliant, they'll like that.'

'And maybe you could write something in it for them?'

'OK. I'll think of something.'

'That's good, I think it would mean a lot to them, both now and when they're older. What's this party you've been invited to?'

I frowned at the receiver. 'Who told you about that?'

'Bres, of course. Just as well he gives me some news, you're about as forthcoming as a rolled-up hedgehog. He said you're mixing with the upper classes. So, what's the story?'

'It's Cecelia's eightieth. She's one of the residents here, she invited me.'

'What's she like, then?'

'She's, you know, interesting, she's had a fascinating life, lived all over the world.'

'I see. What are you going to wear – not those jeans you live in, I hope! Do you need some dosh?'

I thought of how Cecelia would flinch if someone used the word *dosh* in her hearing.

'I don't know what I'm wearing yet.'

'When's the party?'

'In two weeks.'

'You'd better get a move on then, hadn't you? You can never go wrong with a simple skirt and top. Oxford Street would be the place, plenty of chain stores and choice. Dorothy Perkins is always a good bet and pastel colours are nice at your age. So, do you need money?'

'No, it's OK, I haven't been spending much, I've plenty left from what you gave me.'

There was a sudden squawking in the background.

'That's Gregory woken up in a bad mood. No rest for the wicked here, I'd better play nurse with the Paracetamol. I'll want to hear all about the do; it's all right for some, living the life of Riley!'

Whoever Riley was, I muttered, replacing the phone. Bres had looked a little wary when I'd mentioned my invitation to Cecelia's party. He was painting when I told him, perched on his stool, wearing the outsized check shirt he used that was ingrained with daubs from his endeavours. The wide canvas was half-completed, a scene of cargo ships on the River Foyle, the sky a misty stippled grey, the river wide and glinting. The ships were stubby and purposeful; on the quays were blurry flat-capped men, hefting sacks and wheeling barrows.

'Mrs B invited you herself?' he asked, dabbing at the silhouette of a crane.

'Yes, while we were at her dressmaker's.'

'Right, well . . . I suppose there's no harm in it. And you really want to go?'

'Of course, it'll be interesting. Her dressmaker used to work at the Kirov, he knew Nureyev!'

Bres wiped his brush on a rag and stuck it behind his ear. He turned on his stool, looking at me over the top of the rimless glasses he needed for close work. 'Herself and yourself seem to be getting on great guns, what with the drawing and afternoon tea and trips out and now birthday invites.'

'I know she can be a bit offhand, but I like her. She's keen on my drawings, she's asked me to do a special one of her.' I'd been going to show him the ring Cecelia had bought me but something in his voice made me hold back the information. I had a disturbing sensation of things sliding, out of my control.

Bres stood and patted my arm. 'She's a woman of taste, then. Don't be getting a liking for rich food though, will you? Your old granda can't run to foie gras and the like, the scran is simple *chez* Monsieur Bres. Isn't that awful news about the twins getting sick? It was all your poor mother needed after the year she's been having.'

'Terrible,' I agreed, thinking of the party and the jade-green velvet dress I'd seen in the window of a charity shop in Gloucester Road that Gina had told me about. My mother's suggestion of pastels was far from what I had in mind. Impressed by a recent TV screening of *Breakfast at Tiffany's*, I was planning the gamine Audrey Hepburn look. I pictured Luca's gaze at the revelation of a sophisticated little Marti. Turning away, I caught a glimpse of myself in the mirror over the fireplace and saw a slither of shiftiness in my eyes, like a fleeting trace of cloud that made me feel emboldened and uneasy.

When I arrived the following day to sketch Cecelia, Wilhelm let me in, his face half-covered in shaving foam, razor in one hand. He was wearing just tattered khaki shorts, hanging low on his skinny hips and it struck me that I'd seen more male flesh in recent weeks than I had in the whole of my life. Beatrice was idling in the door of her room, eating pastries from a plate. She had on a sundress, a skimpy blue and white striped cotton shift with slender straps; it showed abundant, freckled cleavage. Her wiry light-brown hair was caught up in a clip, with strands floating on her forehead and neck.

'Want one?' she asked, proffering the plate.

I took a triangular pastry and bit into a mixture of almonds, honey and pistachios. 'Delicious,' I said. 'Where did you buy them?'

She laughed, a merry, light chuckle. 'I made them, silly. The best food is home-made, not bought from posh shops, like Luca believes!'

Wilhelm reached for one, and swallowed it in one bite. As he reached past me I caught a whiff of rank armpits.

'You don't mind eating at Luca's expense though . . . or should I say Cecelia's,' he teased Beatrice.

'No one should look a gift horse in the mouth.' Beatrice licked her fingers and devoured another triangle, groaning with delight. 'What more can anyone want; a hot day, a hot lover and ambrosial confectionery?' She placed another pastry halfway into her mouth and leaned forward to Wilhelm, who stepped towards her and took the other half between his lips.

I watched, fascinated, as they twisted their heads, mock snarling, tearing the pastry in two, Wilhelm's shaving foam transferring to Beatrice's cheeks. Then Wilhelm flung his razor to the floor, pushed Beatrice back into her room and slammed the door. I watched the hairs on my arms rise in a cool rush.

I could hear Luca chatting as I walked along the hallway, and Cecelia's light laugh. My heart lifted; I had been hoping that he would be in that morning. They presented a cosy picture as I entered, sitting at their tapestries, stitching away in the sun which cast a mild, butterscotch glow through the high window, with Daphne curled behind Cecelia, a paw covering her eyes. Unlike Wilhelm, Luca was fully dressed and elegant, in black jeans and the whitest of white shirts with a mandarin collar and sleeves rolled up. Cecelia had on a black silk blouse over white trousers. I had become fascinated by light and shade, positive and negative at that time, and I wondered whether they had organized the *chiaroscuro* patterning deliberately. A small pile of birthday invitations had been completed, including one for me. Luca had written mine and I saw him observing me as I read the bold black pen strokes.

'You must forgive the fact I have printed, little Marti,' he said to me. 'I have dreadful handwriting. Musical notes make sense to me, not the written word.'

'No problem,' I said. 'I wasn't expecting a written invite as well.'

'Things must be done properly,' Cecelia declared, tucking her needle in. 'Now, Luca darling, are you going to deliver these while Martina sketches? You needn't post Randolph's, he phoned to say he's calling in today after the dentist.'

Luca pulled a face. 'I'm definitely going out, then. I will see you in a while, *amorin*.' He swept up the envelopes, bent and kissed Cecelia's cheek, blew a kiss to me and was gone.

'Really, men can be such difficult creatures! One has to spend so much time humouring them!' Cecelia was smiling, using the arms of her chair to propel herself upwards. 'Yet,' she said, smoothing her blouse, 'life without them is an arid business, so what is one to do?'

'Keep lots of pets, take up jigsaws?' I suggested. 'Knit toy animals for Oxfam? That's what Gina says she does on long evenings when she's tired of her own company.' I was still looking at my invitation, examining Luca's script. Later, I would trace my fingers along the letters, exhilarated, my cup full.

Cecelia laughed and grimaced. 'Ye gods, I'd rather curl up and die!' She clasped her hands in front of her. 'I was so, so lucky to meet my dear Luca. I think that if I hadn't, I would have given up on the world, it would have had nothing more to offer me. I used to wake in the morning and dread the long, yawning day ahead. There are people, Martina, who are absolutely not built for solitude and I am one of them. I need company just as flowers need sunlight.'

I knew what she meant by waking up and dreading the day. I had felt like that for weeks after my father died and the sensation still ambushed me unexpectedly, bleak moments of staring into emptiness: the shadow, the misted negative.

She touched my arm, apparently reading my mind. 'Meeting Luca taught me a lesson I knew and had forgotten: that everything changes and changes oneself. You must remember that, too.'

Perhaps it was her consideration for me or the quiet inti-macy of the diamond-shaped library where she had arranged for me to sketch her with the Salviati perfume bottle but, as I started to draw, I told her about the dreadful idea that had lodged in my mind and that I couldn't erase. The seed of it had been planted a few nights before when, reading the evening paper, I had come across the story of a woman who had been pronounced dead but had regained consciousness as she was being removed by the undertaker. The terrible image of my father not being dead as he was dispatched at the crematorium had been tormenting me ever since.

'I can't stop thinking about it,' I told Cecelia. 'Mistakes obviously get made, don't they? What if he was still alive and deeply unconscious but no one could tell?'

'You poor girl,' Cecelia said, 'I thought you've been even paler than usual. What a terrible burden to be carrying, I'm surprised you can do anything, let alone draw.'

'I know it sounds crazy.'

'Not at all. Now, first of all, did the paper say what had happened to this woman to render her unconscious?'

'I think it said she'd had a bad reaction to a drug.'

'Well, there you are, entirely special circumstances where the body had shut down as a protective reaction. It may be that these awful things do happen incredibly rarely but your father was killed in an accident, you said. There's no chance that a mistake would be made in a situation like that, where he died in his car.'

I concentrated on the shapes before me, the play of light on Cecelia's hair and the diamond brooch on her collar, the shadow of her arm on the pale wall behind. 'You really think so?'

'Yes, absolutely,' Cecelia said firmly. 'You have only been having these awful thoughts because you have an artist's sensitivity and imagination and because of your loss. You must throw them away and be sensible. Your father would-n't want you to suffer in that way. Have you mentioned this to anyone else?'

I wiped the palms of my hands on my jeans. 'No. I wouldn't have talked to my grandfather about it because it would upset him.'

'Well, that's very adult and wise of you. Now, you must promise me that you won't entertain such horrible thoughts again.'

I told her I would try not to and continued sketching for a few minutes, the only sound a deep purr from somno-lent Daphne. I felt a relief and release that freed my pencil, set it flowing across the paper. We were inter-rupted by the arrival of Randolph, whose heavy tread made the china vases in the hallway vibrate. He shouted that he was taking some painkillers, would be with her in a jiffy.

'Are you there then, Cissy?' his deep, rumbling voice soon called. 'Some half-nude dimpled nymph let me in. Are you running a knocking shop as well now?' He appeared in the doorway, poking the carpet with a silver-topped cane. 'Oh, I see, a drawing class. Who are you, then?' he asked me. 'Another of the multitude of hangers-on?'

'Stop being so insufferable, Randolph.' Cecelia leaned and flicked his arm with a finger. 'This is my friend Martina, who is very talented.'

'Really.' He pointed with his stick at the Salviati bottle. 'Well, I hope she keeps her eyes and fingers on her pencils.

Who's that curvaceous, long-haired gipsy beauty in a bath towel?'

'Her name is Beatrice. She's staying here for a while.'

'Of course she is. Strange time of day to be bathing, I'd have thought. Luca Gonzi's circus, never a dull moment! By the way, what's happening to the west rooms, there's a bloody great bath that looks like a swimming pool standing in the middle of the floor.'

'They're being renovated and redecorated for Luca and that is a Jacuzzi.'

'He's already got a perfectly good room and bathroom, I thought.'

'We decided to make some alterations. Luca needs a quiet environment to compose and practise in.'

'Must be costing you a pretty penny.'

Cecelia frowned. 'That's my business, thank you.'

Randolph winced. 'This bloody tooth is murder. So where is lover-boy, then?'

'Luca has gone to deliver invitations to my party. Yours is here for you, although if you carry on in this appalling, hectoring fashion, I might have to revoke it.'

Randolph was a giant of a man with a florid complexion, well over six foot and big-built with a barrel chest. He was dressed in the kind of outfit that many older men wore in that area of London: mustard-coloured cords, neatly pressed, check shirt with a silk scarf at the neck and olive-green tweed jacket. I found that Rupert Bear always came to mind when I saw one of them.

'Can't come to the party, I'm afraid, Cissy. I have to visit Andrew Liddington in Monte. He's a creaking gate anyway and now he's been told he's got some ghastly disease with not long to go, so I'd better head off before he snuffs it.'

Cecelia looked disappointed but not, I thought, too much so. Maybe she was relieved that Randolph and Luca wouldn't be squaring up to each other over the birthday cake; I could imagine that when they were in a room together it might feel crowded. I was glad that he couldn't come; I had taken an instant dislike to him and his spiteful comments about Luca.

It was while we were in the drawing-room having tea and cake (coffee-and-walnut from Fortnum's) that Randolph spotted the empty space on the mantelpiece. He was a man who liked to keep on the move, roaming the room with his plate in his hand, gazing out of the window, peering at photographs and paintings. He stopped at the fireplace, nibbling a piece of walnut and coughed.

'Where's the Chinese snuffbox, Cissy? It's not here. Have you put it in another room?' He rocked on his heels, turning to stare at her.

'No, it should be there.' Cecelia put her cup down and went over to the mantelpiece. 'Oh, it's gone,' she said vaguely, her voice fluttery.

'Very perceptive of you. There's just the space where it should be. When did you last see it?'

'I'm not sure. I think it was there last week when the fire-screen was being cleaned. Perhaps it's been moved; Luca might have put it away for safekeeping because we've had the workmen in, decorating and so on. Yes, I'm sure that will be it.' She put a hand to her cheek and rubbed at the skin.

Randolph shook his head, making a clicking sound in the back of his throat. 'Oh Cissy, Cissy, you'll never learn, will you? One of those toerags will have taken it; you won't see it again. Just like six months ago when the daguerreotype vanished from the dining-room. Some other circus clowns were here then, weren't they – others from Mr Gonzi's choice troupe of friends.'

He was shaking his head, thudding his cane down, coughing. Cecelia went to the window and pleated a curtain between her fingers. I was beginning to know her reactions; when she was upset her hands trembled and danced, fingers twitching up and down, a movement that suddenly revealed her age and frailty. I found it hard to watch. I started to stack crockery on the tray; I wanted to go but didn't know how to leave the room. Neither of them seemed to hear me.

'You must call the police, Cissy,' Randolph growled, 'get this properly investigated. You can't let this go by, a valuable object vanishing.'

'I'll think about it,' Cecelia said, keeping her back to him. 'I'll speak to Luca.'

'You're a fool, Cissy, you know that, don't you? The man's making a complete idiot of you. You were better off on your own, at least your home was safe, your lovely things.'

'What would you know about me being on my own? What do you know of my grey, drab days and nights, my despairing solitude? A life without affection is a sad existence.' She spoke quietly, almost as if to herself, settling the curtain back, aligning the folds with her thin fingers. 'Do give my best to Andrew when you see him, he was very kind to me that time I ricked my ankle in Hyderabad. Say hello to Monte for me, too.' She gave a kind of backward wave. 'I think you'd better go now, your tooth must be hurting.'

Randolph rapped his cane against the brass fender of the fireplace. 'You're as stubborn as a mule. At least get an inventory done. I'll ring Martins and ask him to arrange it.'

'Very well, yes, if it will keep you happy.'

Randolph exhaled loudly and strode out, flat-footed, leaving the door swinging.

'I rather think these curtains might have moth-holes, how ghastly,' Cecelia murmured. 'Time they were replaced, anyway. I shall arrange for some samples.'

'I hope you find your snuffbox,' I said.

She walked over to her tapestry, gazed down at it and smoothed her palm across the fine threads of a lily. 'I'm sorry about that tiring little scene, families are such a dreadful drag at times,' she said politely, sounding exhausted.

I knew I was being courteously dismissed. I picked up the tray and left it in the kitchen on my way out.

9

Once a week I helped Gina clean out the birdbaths, of which there were twelve throughout the garden, positioned near feeding-tables and nesting-boxes so that, as Gina put it, the birds could snack, shower and sleep. My favourite was a wide basin with a blue interior propped on top of a tall, lichen-draped stone column with tiny birds etched on it; I thought of it as the birds' swimming pool and when I mentioned this to Gina she immediately named it 'Larks' Lido'. The birds dive-bombed it in the mornings and early evenings with much wing-flapping, sending spray flying. We threw handfuls of decayed leaves, breeze-blown petals and green sludge into the bushes, then blasted the bowls clean with a hosepipe.

'I hear you were at one of Cecelia's soirées,' Gina said. 'I don't know how talented Luca is; she certainly spends enough time trying to persuade anyone who'll listen that he's gifted.'

'Maybe she's right.'

Gina snorted and chucked a snail into the rhododen-drons. 'What an idiot the woman is, entertaining that poodle-faker.'

'That what?'

It was a baking day, no wisp of cloud, just the unrelent-ing sun. Gina wiped her brow, smearing dust across it.

'It's an expression my mother used. It means a man who's taking advantage of a woman; you know, making up to her like a pet poodle and being cosseted and indulged. Your grandfather thinks that too, I'll bet.'

'He doesn't have a high opinion of Luca.'

'Yes, well, he's lived, he's probably seen it all before, or something like.'

'Is it hot today or is the Pope a Catholic?' Bres was coming towards us, bearing an ice-cream cornet in each hand, his straw trilby at a rakish angle. 'I brought the labourers some refreshment, plain vanilla to cater for all tastes.'

We licked eagerly at the ice cream while he surveyed our handiwork.

'You're going great guns. Marti, you're getting a hint of a tan, you're almost looking healthy now, like a young girl should.' He walked his fingers across my head. 'Now, you were deep in talk, your heads together. What's the word on the streets?'

Gina explained our conversation, belching loudly as she swiftly finished her cornet.

'Now, I've never heard that term, *poodle-faker*,' Bres said. 'We used to say that someone who'd been conned had been *sold a pup*. I agree with you though, Gina; the lady is keeping strange company. Marti, what's your opin-ion? You've been spending a bit of time with Mrs B and her chums.'

I squinted, crunching on my cornet. I hated hearing this

criticism but I tried to sound nonchalant. 'People might think that Luca is taking advantage but that's not all of the story, is it?'

Gina blew hair from her forehead. 'Meaning?'

I closed my eyes for a moment, to get the words right. Somehow, I felt it was important and that I owed it to Cecelia and Luca. Someone had to be on their side. 'I think Cecelia is really fond of him. He makes her happy, makes her laugh. She says she was terribly lonely until she met him and he completely changed her life. That has to count for a lot, doesn't it?'

Bres took a handkerchief from his pocket and dabbed his brow. 'It does, Marti, it does. Nobody would want to see her lonesome. But that doesn't make what's happening right. There's something upsetting about a person being used.'

The palms of my hands were sweaty despite the ice cream. I felt a foggy confusion that made me want to contradict him. 'Cecelia gets offended by people saying things about her and Luca and trying to interfere. She says that she doesn't see why it's anyone else's business.'

Bres looked at me, nodded. I could see him weighing his words, rising and falling softly on his feet. 'Tell me this much,' he said, adjusting the brim of his hat to stop the sun getting in his eyes. 'Would you say that Mr Gonzi is fond of Mrs B? Would *he* be lonely without *her*?'

I heard Luca's endearments: *amorin, namrata* and recalled the way he had handled the flowers he'd bought for Cecelia, the glances that had passed between him and Wilhelm. I thought of how tenderly my father had looked at my mother, the understanding, needing no explanation, that he would never have allowed anyone to say a word against her. And yet now that I was in thrall I wouldn't agree to any fault-finding.

'He might be, you might be misjudging him, you know.'

Bres looked at me, tilting back his hat. 'Hmm, well, when all's said and done, Mrs B can't stop people having eyes and ears and opinions. It's a free country.'

Gina nodded and turned the hose back on, sending a jet of water spraying. We finished our task while Bres went off to check the window-cleaner who, he said, was as slippery as an eel and lower than a snake's belly. As Gina rewound the hose she breathed deeply and smiled.

'You know, in most world religions heaven has been depicted as a garden. I hope that if there is a heaven and I go there, it's a garden like this on a day just like today.'

I thought of my father and wondered whether he might be lying by a pond in paradise or sniffing a divine honey-suckle. He had to be careful not to burn in the sun so I hoped that if he was in a heavenly garden he had plenty of high-factor cream and a hat. I said as much to Gina and she replied that there would be no problem because the sun that shone in a heavenly garden wouldn't burn, which I realized was obvious and comforting, too.

We passed through the clematis arch by the statue of Pan and there were Luca, Cecelia and Wilhelm sitting on the lawn, examining glossy brochures. Cecelia was seated on a small rattan chair, holding a yellow parasol that glowed with a buttery light. The two men were on either side of her on the grass, Wilhelm in swimming-trunks, lying on his stomach, Luca in Bermuda shorts and sleeveless shirt. A bottle of sun-tan cream lay between them, the cap flipped back and a trickle of the glossy lotion trailing. I was reminded of a painting, a Matisse or Degas, that I had seen in the National Gallery, with such a trio relaxing in another era.

'How lovely to see you both!' Cecelia called. 'Do come and join us, Beatrice is bringing some refreshments.'

'I'd better get on, I've loads to do,' Gina said gruffly.

'Oh, we won't detain you for long, the workers surely must have their rest!' Cecelia gestured at the grass. She was full of smiles and spoke so lightly and gracefully that Gina shrugged and sat, propping her back against the coiled hose. I knelt down by Luca. He had a tattoo that I hadn't noticed before, on his left shoulder, a small circle of yellow and red bands with blue and green spirals within.

'Do you like it?' he asked me, seeing me looking. 'I just had it done.' He ran his fingers over it and smiled at me.

I thought the colours too garish. 'It's interesting,' I said. 'What does it mean?'

'Wilhelm, what's it called again, the tattoo?'

Wilhelm yawned and continued reading his brochure. I could see photos of beaches and swimming pools. 'It's a triskele.'

'That's right. It's Celtic, represents life. Wilhelm's mother is from Brittany, that's why he chose it. He has one too. We have a bond now, eh Willi? Brothers of the tattoo.' Luca stretched a foot out and nudged Wilhelm's fingers, making his brochure slip.

'You boys!' Cecelia said indulgently. 'What will you think of next!'

Luca leaned up, stroked her hair back and whispered in her ear, making her giggle and tap her hands on her lap.

Gina glanced at me, blinking rapidly. I had to look down, disguising a blush.

'What's this, then, Cecelia?' Gina reached for one of the brochures. 'Are you planning a holiday?'

'Yes, indeed!' Cecelia sat up straighter. 'Luca and I wish to go somewhere warm this winter. I can't bear the cold – never could actually, but especially now. I want to be away for at least a month. Beatrice has kindly said that she will look after the flat for us, feed Daphne and so on.'

'Very thoughtful of her,' Gina said. 'Where are you think-ing of going?' She looked at Luca as she spoke.

He gestured towards Cecelia. 'It is the lady's choice,' he said.

'Well, yes, I suppose it would be, as she'll be paying,' Gina said airily.

'Refreshment time!' Beatrice called, arriving noiselessly in bare feet with a loaded silver tray. She was dressed in a green-and-white bikini with a matching sarong tied loosely at her hips, accentuating her Rubens-like curves. Luca rose to help her, fetching a wooden table, checking that its legs were steady. She set the tray down clumsily, pink liquid splashing from a tall glass jug in which floated slices of cucumber and sprigs of mint. There were also little crystal bowls heaped with strawberries and cherries.

'How super, Beatrice, how thoughtful of you,' Cecelia said, folding her parasol.

'Not at all.' Beatrice smiled. 'It is thirsty work, choosing a holiday. Thank you,' she said to Luca as he checked again the table's stability. She shot a look at Wilhelm. 'It's so nice that some men have manners.'

Wilhelm turned a page and blew her a kiss, laughing. He

ran a finger down the back of her bare leg and she moved away, tucking stray hair up into the dragonfly-shaped clip that rode the back of her head.

'I shall be mother,' Luca said, pouring drinks. 'Everyone for a Pimm's?' He handed the glasses round, giving one to me. 'It's OK,' he said, winking at me, 'Beatrice makes it mainly lemonade, there's not enough alcohol in it to get a little Marti drunk.'

I sipped, liking the mint and ice but the drink itself tasted like a weak cough linctus. I was trying to take in this news of a holiday in the autumn. It was anticipating a time when I wouldn't be at Dauncey, near to Luca and I didn't want to contemplate the future.

'Health and happiness to all,' Cecelia toasted, drinking deeply and pointing to a brochure. 'I do rather like the idea of the Solomon Islands, they are so lovely. But I've never been to Tahiti and that's a real draw, too.'

'Darling, you went to the Solomons with Olly. I think this time we should head somewhere neither of us has been. Then it is special to us, we make our own history.'

Luca was sitting by her chair. He looked up at her, wrinkling his nose. She touched his cheek. Gina leaned across me for a strawberry, whispering, '*woof woof!*' and I took a gulp of drink, coughing as some went up my nose.

'That's true, Luca,' Cecelia smiled. 'Tahiti, then?'

'Mmm, I envy you. That sea looks so blue!' Beatrice said, gazing at the pictures. '*Here you will find beauty, romance, and, above all, sheer escapism. Imagine discovering your own secret paradise – a world of crystal-clear aquamarine waters and deserted white-sand beaches, just waiting to be explored in a heaven on earth where your dreams will come true,*' she read aloud in a breathless voice, dabbing her fingers into her drink and trailing them across her throat.

'Yes, you will be in paradise and we lesser mortals will be toiling.' Wilhelm drained his glass and poured himself another Pimm's. He didn't offer to refill anyone else's glass, but grabbed a handful of cherries and ate them swiftly, the juice running down his chin.

'Goodness! Are you in danger of getting a job then, Wilhelm?' Gina asked.

'I have my own plans, my own travels,' he said sharply, spitting cherry stones behind him.

'Beatrice will miss you when you go away, won't you, Bea?' Luca said softly, twitching the hem of her sarong.

'Yes, but I will have to be brave and bear it. You'll come back to me, won't you, Willi, you'll come back to your little goose?' Beatrice rested her glass on her cleavage.

Wilhelm turned to Cecelia. 'So, when will you book the tickets for Tahiti?'

'Two tickets to Tahiti; it sounds like a film, one with Bette Davis in.' Cecelia smiled. 'We will go and book tomorrow; we have various bits of important business to complete tomorrow, don't we, Luca darling?'

'We have,' he confirmed, raising his glass to her.

A glance passed between Beatrice and Wilhelm. It seemed to be an afternoon for meaningful looks and hints. Gina cast her eyes heavenwards and hoisted her hose. Some people, she commented, had real work to do. I was woozy from my drink, however light the alcohol. I lay back on the grass; some wisps of cirrus cloud had arrived, coiling from the east, and I scanned them for shapes. I saw what might be a chimney and a lion's mane but no sign of what I was seeking. My mother had told the Calamities that Daddy might be riding a cloud, looking down on them, but I couldn't make him out, even though I stared so hard my eyes ached.

'I think little Marti needs a lullaby after her afternoon tipple, she looks like a sleepyhead,' Luca said. He came and sat beside me on the grass and started to play his guitar, singing softly;

The summer wind came blowing in from across the sea,
It lingered there, and touched your hair and walked with me.
All summer long we sang a song and strolled on golden sand
Two sweethearts, and the summer wind.

'There,' he said, lightly placing a hand over my eyes, 'a ballad just for you, little Marti, to make you dream sweetly.'

As he repeated: *All summer long, we sang a song and strolled on golden sand, two sweethearts, and the summer wind*, I kept my eyes shut, still feeling the impression of his warm, dry palm and the cool band of the bracelet he was wearing. In my heart brewed a tempest of confusion, delight and fear. I saw flying red and gold stars fill the afternoon sky.

The charity shop in Gloucester Road was called Bits and Bobs and to my delight the dress I had spotted was still in the window. The air inside was thick with the fustiness of tired fabrics and the pungent aroma of scented candles. After a fit of sneezing, I asked the ancient, stooped man who was fussing with a stand of greetings cards to fetch the dress for me. I squeezed into the tiny changing cubicle, pulled the faded yellow curtain across and examined my find, thrilled to read Nina Ricci on the label. It was jade silk, lined with grey and with a grey velvet bow under the bust and a trim in the same velvet around the neckline and hem. It smelled dusty but I could see no marks or tears and the armpits, when I checked them, exhibited no yellowing – Gina had advised me to carry out this particular scrutiny. I reckoned it was unworn or perhaps worn only once. I tried the dress on. It was almost a perfect fit. The side zip was a little sticky but I managed to ease it up and down. I looked in the mottled mirror and swept my hair up; I was pleased by my pale, willowy reflection. The dress instantly created an older, worldlier Martina, and also a Martina who seemed suddenly and gratifyingly taller.

On the side wall of the cubicle was a cloth picture of a giraffe in bright yellows and reds, marked out in centimetres, a measuring chart for children. I stood against it and marked the place with my finger. Turning, I was thrilled to see that I had grown by almost two centimetres and that Bres hadn't, after all, shrunk my jeans in his machine.

As I took the dress to the till, I noticed a hideous painting of white unicorns prancing through a foaming river with silver fish leaping around them, but I stopped to examine the frame, which was a beautiful acorn-coloured birch and unblemished. It would make a fitting surround for my portrait of Cecelia with scent bottles, which I had been working on for hours and planned to give her as a birthday gift.

My two purchases came to just under fifteen pounds; buoyed up by my bargain I walked along the sunny streets, wedging the awkward frame under my right arm. It was one of my favourite London days; balmy rather than hot, with a light breeze and a clear blue sky, a washed inky-blue. I was envisaging Cecelia's party, wondering whether to buy ribbon or a clip to secure a knot in my hair, imagining what Luca would be wearing, when a black taxi swept in beside me and Luca opened the door, leaning through.

'Hop in, little Marti,' he said, 'you look weighed down.'

I stammered thanks, thinking that this seemed more than coincidence, as if I had summoned him through my longings. I clambered in beside him, banging my knee on the frame. He took the picture, looked at it and winced.

'I know, I know,' I told him. 'I bought it for the frame, to reuse.'

He nodded. 'I see. Thank goodness, I thought you had suddenly developed kitsch tendencies!'

I gazed at the horses, their flaring nostrils and high tails. They looked even worse in the filtered interior light. 'You never know, though, it might be valuable in forty years time – all kinds of styles become trendy again. My mother has a pair of Loon pants from 1972 that she's keeping for when they're back in fashion.'

Luca had taken an aerosol spray from his pocket and was tilting his head back, applying it his throat. 'Excuse me,' he said, rubbing his neck with smooth upward strokes, 'I am going to a rehearsal and I find that my vocal chords get a little taut when I am nervous.'

I couldn't imagine him ever being anything other than brimming with confidence. He looked completely at ease, sitting back with his lute across his thighs. I was scrunched against the seat, the object of my affections almost too near, the proximity too sudden and unexpected.

'Why don't you come with me?' he asked, gently flicking my earlobe. 'It's in a church, just a couple of minutes away. Yes, do come; it would be good to have your opinion of the acoustics. It won't take long and then we can taxi home with your Old Master. What have you got in the bag?'

He plucked enquiringly at the top but I pulled it against me. I wanted to keep the dress a secret so that he would be impressed at the party.

'It's to do with Cecelia's birthday,' I said, 'and not to be seen until then.'

'Ooh, little Marti, you have hidden depths!' He put out a long arm and tucked my fringe to the side with one finger, resting the tip for a moment against my temple.

I started, an involuntary reflex and pretended that my leg had gone to sleep. 'Hasn't everyone got hidden depths?' I asked with a coolness I didn't feel. Then, because he made me feel so confused and exposed and because my senses were swimming, I blurted out, 'Did Cecelia find the snuff-box?'

He drew himself up, gave me a sharp glance. 'What snuffbox?'

'The Chinese one, in the sitting-room; Randolph Smythe noticed that it was missing from the mantelpiece.'

'Did he really?' Luca touched his bent thumb between his eyebrows. 'Cecelia hasn't mentioned it, actually. We've been very busy with the party arrangements and the reno-vations. Randolph is such a bore, always interfering. He hasn't got enough to entertain him. Maybe he'll stay in

Monte this time, find something or someone else to bother. But nothing can displease me today, little Marti; all alterations and redecorations were completed this morning and the workmen have gone to annoy other people. I have beautiful accommodation where I can fully develop my talents. Ah, here we are!'

The church we entered was made of a beautiful pale stone. I recognized the Gothic style that Victorians were so keen on, complete with flying buttresses and parapets. I was disappointed, though, to see that modern doors with huge squares of plate-glass had been fitted between the foyer and the body of the church and I winced as we passed through them. Inside, my spirits revived; the interior was lofty and welcomingly cool with a hint of mildew, two tall stained-glass windows rose up behind the altar, a tranquil blend of blues and greens. There was an echoing scrape and clatter, plucking of strings and hoot of scales as a number of musicians drew chairs into a circle, opened instrument cases and began to tune up. A plump-faced man in a purple shirt and dog collar turned as we walked up the aisle and rubbed his hands together dramatically.

'Ah, we have our solo performer! Greetings, Luca!'

Luca touched his hand in a high five and introduced me as little Marti, saying that this was Canon Peregrine.

'But do call me Perry,' the canon said, 'we have no formality here. Little Marti is your name? It's unusual.'

'No, Luca calls me that, no one else does.'

'Ah, an endearment, I see. He must be fond of you, he misses his little sisters in Malta, you know.'

I warmed to this canon, smiled at him.

'Do you mind if I run through my piece first? I have an

appointment.' Luca was taking his lute out and holding it up to the light. It was a command, not a question, and the canon fluttered his fingers saying of course, it was time to crack on.

An oboe and recorder accompanied Luca as he sang. Perry sat next to me as the pure, clear sound floated upwards.

The sweetness of thy love divine
My sinful soul assuages
And gives my life that peace I crave
Although I do not merit thy regard.

Perry rocked a little on his chair, leaning forward.

'This concert will be televised; it will be wonderful for the church appeal. It's so good of Luca to give up his time,' he whispered to me. 'We need to do major works on the roof, the water seepage is simply dreadful.'

I nodded, looking at him, realizing as I examined his rounded head and glasses that he was one of the men in boxer shorts I had seen in the gardens late at night at Dauncey, the one being given the piggyback. I glanced down, suppressing a giggle, focusing on the music:

My spirit rises as I am bathed in your golden gifts. I
am planted by streams of water and prosper in your
kindly sight.

Just then I was the one who was bathed and prospering, in the company and view of my beloved. I gazed at Luca; he had his eyes closed and was flexing the fingers of his right hand as the oboe played. Sunlight was dancing on the blue and green glass over the altar, depicting the journey into Egypt, St Joseph striding with a staff beside his pregnant wife. I wanted the gilded moment to go on for ever.

The traffic was slow on the way back to Dauncey. The taxi crept along, halting for minutes at a time. Luca sighed and said that although he loved London, he sometimes missed Malta: the simplicity, the outdoor life, the air quality.

'This air is not so good for my lungs, for my pipes,' he said, tapping his chest.

'What made you leave Malta?' I burbled, overjoyed at this opportunity to talk to him, yet simultaneously longing to wrench open the taxi door and flee.

'No prospects: the usual emigrant story. My family fish for a living, have done for generations. I had greater aspirations; there was no chance in Malta of development, of a singing career. One of my older brothers became a waiter in a hotel, one of my sisters a chambermaid. I had no intention of following their careers. I busked for a while in Paris and here, rather than put on a uniform and clear up after others.'

'Do you miss your family?'

He yawned, sucking in air. 'Of course, yes. Actually, Cecelia has kindly said that she will invite my mother and sister to come next summer. And there is a singing programme in Rome that I will be attending in the winter; I will probably pay a flying visit to them after that, although I don't like to leave Cecelia for too long.' He leaned forward, tapped the glass. 'Hey, driver man, I've got things to do. Surely you must know some handy side streets, you look like a guy with know-how!'

He and the driver started to banter. I watched him, drinking him in, wanting to absorb some of his assurance, his ease in dealing with the world.

When I arrived back that afternoon I found Bres in his room, hurriedly packing a bag. As he stuffed socks and shirts in he told me that my mother had come down with mumps, had a high temperature and could barely lift her head off the pillow. Sister Tricia was trying to help but Ursula and Gregory were still poorly and cranky so extra measures were called for.

'And I've had mumps, so I'm in no danger,' he said, looking around. 'Have you seen my reading-glasses?'

'On the window ledge,' I pointed.

He tucked them into the pocket of his shirt, alongside the black Biro that always sat in there.

'Now you'll be OK here on your own, won't you? There's plenty of grub in the fridge and freezer and I've left Gina's, Righty's and Tullamore Joe's phone numbers for you, they're pinned up in the kitchen.'

'How long are you going for?' I brought him his brush and comb from the dressing-table.

'I don't rightly know, pet. At least a couple of days, I'd say. Mumps are severe for adults, that why you don't want to be anywhere near them. And there's no cure, you see, apart from painkillers. You poor mother will just have to wait it out. She needed this like a hole in the head. I don't know, it never rains but it pours. She was worried about me leaving you here but I told her needs must when the devil drives; you're a sensible girl, you know plenty of people and you'll be fine.'

'Of course I will,' I confirmed.

He patted my arm. 'I'll ring you every morning and evening, let's say at 8 a.m. and p.m., just to check and give you a bulletin. Oh, and Mrs Buchanan gave me a note for you – I told her I'm having to disappear suddenly – and I let Gina know too.' He scratched his head and looked around again, let out a sigh. 'I think that's it. Now, remember to lock the door at night and switch off the TV. I'd better get my skates on if I'm going to catch the 4.30. Come here and give me a hug.'

I put my arms around him, straightened his collar and licking my thumbs, smoothed down his eyebrows.

'Oh,' he said, 'and there's fifty quid in the tea caddy in the cupboard over the toaster, in case of need or dire emergency.'

When he had gone, whirling out of the door with hat in one hand, bag in the other, I walked around the flat. It was quiet and empty, sleepy in the late-afternoon sun. He must have been disturbed with the news from home while he was painting because some of his paint tubes were uncapped and sticky brushes lay on his palette. I secured the paints and cleaned the brushes, wiping them dry and standing them in their rack. The painting looked almost finished; I could see that he had been adding the names of one of the grain mills on the quays; DOHE was all it said so far.

I poured an orange juice and opened Cecelia's note.

Dear Martina, your grandfather has explained that he has to leave for a few days. You are welcome to visit us at any time so please do not be lonely. With best wishes, CB.

In my room, I opened a drawer and took out the dozens of sketches I had been making of Luca, both from life and memory: Luca in the garden, in the flat, walking, at the restaurant and at the soirée, at the harpsichord, sewing his tapestry, holding his lute, on his mobile phone, through the window of the barber's shop. Now that Bres had gone away, I could put them up on my wall and study them properly. I stuck them to the wall opposite my bed, then propped myself against my pillow and gazed at them. The best, I decided, was the one I had done at the musical soirée, probably because the subject had sat more or less still. The shading was tightly executed, his forehead and chin reflecting the light gratifyingly. I had used a soft chamois leather to work on the skin tones, the first time I had tried this and I liked the refinement it added and the way it enhanced the contours of his cheeks. I drifted into a pleasant reverie set at some time in years to come; myself and Luca living in Cecelia's flat with Cecelia herself a benign absence, possibly somewhere abroad. I had a successful portrait business and the library had become my studio. Luca had a recording contract and performances booked throughout the year; we frequently travelled together around the world. At home in the evenings he sang or played to me while I framed portraits. The richness of our shared talents nourished us both.

I glanced at Cecelia's note again and felt a twinge of guilt for removing her so effectively from the picture. I reassured myself that I had been thinking about the future, when she would be very old or possibly dead; in fact, I reasoned, with her true fondness for me and appreciation of my talent, she would like nothing more than that I would be Luca's soul companion when she was no longer around.

10

I'm sure that there are textbooks describing the kind of mental state I inhabited during those months at Dauncey. I recall coming across an article in a psychology magazine when I was at university, which dealt with the condition called limerence; in plain English, having a crush or intense romantic desire for someone. I recognized all the details, the descriptions of happiness and anguish, the craving to be near the subject of affection. The need for proximity, it explained, repeated and mirrored childhood bonding. It didn't take much self-analysis for me to realize that my obsession with Luca had been an unconscious attempt to fill the hollow place left by my father's death, Certainly, it had quietened my grief for my father, or maybe just masked it.

Later that evening after Bres had departed, I made beans on toast for tea and ate them watching a soap opera on television. It was odd being on my own but I didn't dislike the experience. I put my feet up on the coffee table and had second helpings of raspberry ice cream. Bres rang on the dot of eight to tell me he had arrived safely, that my mother was still very poorly and in bed and that the twins were starting to mend but tired easily. He said he hoped I wasn't feeling abandoned and I reassured him that I was fine. I didn't mention that I hadn't given him or my struggling family a single thought since he had left. The intense joy and anxiety of my romantic adventure rendered everyone else's existence a sideshow.

After his call I left my dirty dishes in the sink, realizing that no one would know I had failed to wash up. It was only 8.30 and after several hours of my own undiluted company, I felt fidgety. I brushed my teeth, changed my shirt, fluffed my hair out and headed for Cecelia's. I crossed my fingers on the stairs, hoping that Luca would be in. He was, sitting with Cecelia at the small walnut table playing canasta while Beatrice worked on Cecelia's tapestry. There was a hostess trolley in a cherry-coloured wood that I hadn't seen before, containing a bottle of wine in a cooler and little savoury biscuits and cheese straws in bowls.

'Martina, how lovely to see you, I was hoping you would come.' Cecelia smiled. 'I do hope your mother will be well soon.'

'Thanks. Bres just phoned, he's got everything under control. It was nice of you to send me a note.'

Cecelia perused her cards and selected another from a turned-down pack. 'When I was at school I had a teacher who said that "nice" was an overworked word. We had to do exercises filling in other adjectives such as "lovely" and "pleasant". But of course grammar was taught in those days.'

Luca raised his eyebrows at me, shrugged and gestured at the food. 'Help yourself, little Marti and to a drink –

there's a selection of juices down there, in the fridge.'

I opened one of the wooden doors to find a small icebox crammed with cartons and tins of juice; apple, pineapple, orange, mango and tomato. I poured some mango and selected a cheese straw.

'Do you know,' Cecelia said, 'this is the first time I've played canasta for years. I learned it in Biarritz, when I got engaged to Olly. He was hopeless at card games, he didn't have the temperament for them. He showed his emotions too easily.'

'Luca's good, he can maintain an impassive expression,' Beatrice said, smoothing a thread down. 'I'm so hungry, I hope that food will be here soon. Can you pass me a nibble, Marti?'

She took a handful of biscuits, gulping them down with wine. The doorbell rang and I heard Wilhelm shouting he'd get it. Cecelia reached for her purse and gave Luca several twenty-pound notes which he vanished with.

'We're having Thai take-away, Martina,' she told me, her eyes dancing. 'I'm so looking forward to it, I loved the food when we were in Koh Samui.' She put her cards face down carefully. 'Before I met darling Luca, I was living on sandwiches and soup. Solitary eating is so boring; it's the sharing that delights and sparks the appetite. Beatrice, my dear, could you get the plates from the warmer?'

I looked at the tapestry while Beatrice, who was wearing clogs, clumped to the trolley and clattered plates. She had done some stitches in a leaf wrongly and I wondered that she had left them, marring the harmony of the pattern. Watching her ungainly movements, I thought her an unlikely person to be interested in sewing.

I shared the take-away, warm with pleasure as Luca assumed that I would join them and served me a plate of noodles and curried chicken. Wilhelm opened more wine and handed Cecelia a large glass. She picked at her plate, selecting small pieces of meat, then called for a toast.

'Here's to darling Luca's lovely new accommodation,' she said. 'I have arranged a little ceremony for after supper, haven't I, Beatrice?'

Beatrice nodded, tapping the side of her nose at Luca as she quickly spooned up sticky rice.

'You know, Bea dear,' Luca said mildly, 'you don't have to cram in every meal as if you're expecting a famine at any time.'

Beatrice pulled a face at him and continued her rapid progress. She gulped as she ate, sucking in air. She was wearing pink jeans and a T-shirt that showed a bulging midriff and puffy upper arms; she had certainly put on weight.

'Bea believes in reincarnation,' Wilhelm laughed. 'Probably she was starved in a previous life, or maybe she asphyxiated from food going down her windpipe.'

'There's nothing wrong with a healthy appetite,' Beatrice sniffed, topping up her glass.

Cecelia was gazing into the middle distance with a smile on her lips. I wondered if she was drinking too soon after taking her medication. I glanced at Luca as often as I could. He was a delicate eater, pausing between forkfuls, frequently wiping his mouth with a linen napkin. His deft, quick movements were part of his beauty; I had never seen him do anything ungainly. I made myself eat more slowly and place my fork down as I chewed.

'Do you really believe you've lived before?' I asked Beatrice.

'Hmm. I know I have, I've been hypnotized.' Beatrice approached the trolley and helped herself to more satay sauce and dumplings. 'I recalled being a Phoenician princess; I had slaves and beautiful jewellery.'

Wilhelm sniggered. 'Funny how people who remember other lives have never been rubbish-collectors or rat exterminators.'

'There's no point in discussing the subject with you, it's like casting pearls before swine,' Beatrice said airily, collapsing back into her chair.

Luca yawned and hummed, standing and stretching to the ceiling. 'Sometimes,' he said, 'the intellectual calibre of conversation here is too much to bear.' He smiled down at me. 'I bet little Marti could tell us something fascinating, something that would stimulate our brains.'

I looked at him and knew that I must meet the challenge. Luckily for me, in our family we loved to sing and recite poetry at all social occasions. I stood, placing my plate on the trolley, took a breath and recited the poem Bres had taught me many years before and which I had delivered dozens of times. I couldn't look at Luca, of course; I gazed at the sideboard, speaking slowly;

Had I the heavens' embroidered cloths,
Enwrought with golden and silver light,
The blue and the dim and the dark cloths
Of night and light and the half-light,
I would spread the cloths under your feet:
But I, being poor, have only my dreams;

I have spread my dreams under your feet;
Tread softly because you tread upon my dreams.

Luca led the applause when I finished, bowing low to me. 'Bravo, little Marti, bravo!' he said.

'Absolutely, a delightful rendition of WB!' Cecelia echoed.

I smiled, ecstatic, riding high.

When we had finished eating, Cecelia led us all through to the completed rooms, bidding Wilhelm to open champagne and bring it on a tray. He clicked his heels and saluted, saying that her wish was his command. A long red ribbon had been looped across the doors of Luca's rooms, twisted around the handles and finished in a huge bow. Luca laughed, saying now he understood what had been going on behind his back earlier. He bent and kissed Cecelia's cheek. Wilhelm appeared with the champagne and Luca handed glasses around, including a brimming one for me. Cecelia held her hand out to Beatrice, who passed her a pair of scissors.

'I now declare these apartments open and wish my darling Luca much happiness and contentment,' she said, cutting the bow.

We chinked our glasses and drank. I was already floating after a few sips.

'Little Marti, you haven't seen my rooms yet, have you? Let me give you a guided tour.'

Luca threw all the doors open, then put his hand under my elbow and showed me in. Cecelia followed and I was annoyed that we were not going to be alone but somehow relieved, too, as the first room we entered was his bedroom. It had been fitted with slim, ceiling to floor wardrobes; there was a new four-poster bed with a canopy, fitted bookshelves and a wide, sleek TV. A door led us to the adjoining bathroom which now boasted the star-shaped sunken bath/Jacuzzi, with moulded seats and neck rests.

'Look!' Luca pressed a switch and the ceiling above the Jacuzzi danced with pale blue and silver stars, moons and planets.

'It's beautiful!' I exclaimed.

'Yes; it's better in the dark, then you get the full effect,' Luca said. 'Now I can really have the sun in the morning and the moon at night.' He bowed to Cecelia, who was examining her hair in the mirror, smoothing a strand back. 'All thanks to my dear lady, of course.'

'The music studio, darling Luca, show Martina the studio – as an artist that will be of great interest to her.'

Cecelia was wrong; it was the enchanting bathroom I wanted to linger in, under the starry night sky. The studio was a blank space, apart from Luca's instruments, a few leather chairs and a bank of high-tech equipment, glowing with red and green lights.

'I can sing in here at full volume,' he informed me, 'and nothing can be heard outside. It is a place I have always dreamed of, where I can rehearse and perfect.'

'Let's try it,' Cecelia said. 'Do some of your exercises now, Luca, then we will go outside while you continue and we can prove that all is silence without!'

He looked annoyed. 'You know, I am not a performing seal, *namrata*.'

'Oh darling, don't be moody! I'm so pleased and I know I'm showing off a little to Martina but indulge me?' She put a hand on his arm, stroked it.

He shrugged, closed his eyes. I could see the tension in his jaw. Then he suddenly straightened, relaxed his shoulders, rolled on his feet and started humming softly with his mouth closed, gradually opening his lips until he was singing a loud 'ah'. His eyes were still shut. He made a dismissive gesture at us, the 'ah' moving up a note and increasing in volume until his voice filled the room.

Cecelia led me out, closing the door. We stood in the hall, listening only to the sound of laughter on Beatrice's television.

'Wonderful,' Cecelia said, nodding to me, 'just as we hoped, our dearest Luca will have complete privacy.'

I wanted to open the door, sit in one of the leather chairs and listen to him go up and down his scales but Cecelia was leading me away, saying that I must look at the menu for her birthday party. I glanced back at the closed door, gently blew a little kiss from my fingers to it as Cecelia mused that the pleasure of entertaining was one of the joys that did not dim with age.

The morning of Cecelia's birthday was fine, with wisps of cloud and a whisper of breeze. I ran up the stairs to deliver her card; I was saving her present until that evening, when I knew that other people would be giving theirs. Fortunata opened the door to me, mop in hand, but Luca appeared immediately behind her, wearing a striped towelling dressing-gown. His chin had dark stubble and he was bleary-eyed.

'I'm sorry,' I said, flustered, 'have I called too early?' It was half past nine but I felt as if I had made a terrible social *faux pas.* 'It's OK, I brought a card for Cecelia but I can come back later,' I added as Fortunata glided away and he stood, staring at me. It was the first time I had seen him looking jaded.

He gave himself a visible shake. 'Don't be a silly little Marti,' he said. 'The birthday girl is having a treat; breakfast in bed, with champagne, so we are not in our usual routine. Come on in, there are some warm croissants left.'

He led me to Cecelia's bedroom, his long brown legs striding.

'Look who has come with a card for you, *amorin*,' he called.

Cecelia was propped up against her pillows, holding a champagne flute and wearing a green pashmina around her shoulders. She seemed pale and worn, the colour of the wrap draining her face. At first I thought she wasn't well but then I realized that the reason for her pallor was because she had no make-up on; I had only ever seen Cecelia prepared for the public gaze before. Her wispy hair was fluffed out and I saw a brush beside her on the bedside table.

'Martina, how kind of you, you are so thoughtful,' she said, taking the card I proffered. 'Luca, please draw up a chair. Would you like some coffee, fruit, a croissant?'

'A croissant would be lovely, thanks.' I had already eaten a bowl of muesli but the sight of the food on the trolley made me ravenous; there were heaped brioches and croissants, a glistening bowl of apricots, strawberries, cherries and grapes and of course the champagne in an ice-bucket.

'Luca is so kind, he prepared this very special start to the day for me. I was so thrilled when I woke to it all!'

Luca was eating an apricot, neatly and efficiently, placing the stone on a side plate. 'What would you like, little Marti: chocolate, almond or plain croissant?' he asked.

'Almond, please.'

I watched as he expertly flipped a plump oval croissant onto a linen napkin. He then poured me a coffee, adding warm milk.

'*Bon appetit*,' he said. 'Now, birthday girl, can I tempt you to anything else? More champagne?'

'I shouldn't, but go on. I'll take my tablets mid-morning; I can break the rules today of all days.' She opened my card and smiled; 'Matisse, how lovely, thank you. Look at dear Luca's card, it is so exquisite, he had it made specially.'

She reached to the table and handed me a small card with an abstract, woven design that looked like birds intertwined with leaves. I opened it and read: *To my* amorin *Cecelia; age cannot wither her, nor custom stale her infinite variety.*

'The quote is from Antony and Cleopatra,' Cecelia said. 'You do realize you chose one of the tragedies, Luca?'

He raised his eyebrows. 'The poetry is fitting, isn't that all that matters?'

'It's lovely, very delicate,' I said. 'Who's the artist?'

'A guy who works off the Portobello Road. I met him at the gym, of all places. He does commercial and personalized stuff. If I ever make a recording I want him to do the cover.'

He tore the corner off a croissant and started talking to Cecelia about their plans for the day; I heard Harvey Nichols, a hairdresser and Le Gavroche mentioned. I sipped my coffee and wandered into a reverie about a future where Luca wouldn't need to place commissions with a stranger: I was a lauded artist who designed all of his publicity and covers. I pictured evenings when we drank champagne and examined my rough sketches, choosing which ones to use.

My dreaming and the bedside tête à tête were interrupted by a ring at the door and Fortunata coming to Cecelia with a business card, murmuring that a Mrs Cunningham had arrived.

Cecelia looked annoyed and reached for her glasses, shaking them open.

'Oh, this really is too much and on my birthday!' she exclaimed, handing Luca the card. 'The solicitor has sent this inventory person here. It's Randolph's doing, he said he was going to arrange it but I hardly thought today of all days! Show her into the drawing-room for now, Fortunata.'

Luca tutted. 'It is a strange present, *namrata*. Perhaps his little joke; as he cannot be here he wants us to remember him. The whole idea is ridiculous and I don't like the implication. After all, I wish as much as you to keep all your beautiful things safe and I would say that these days it is more my business than his.' He stroked her hand. 'Shall I tell this woman to go away?' He stood, as if expecting her agreement.

Cecelia bit her lip and removed her glasses, dropping them so they almost fell off the bed. I picked them up and folded them, replacing them on the table next to her tissues. They were as light and fragile as her hands.

'Maybe they did write to arrange the visit,' she said doubtfully. 'I've been so busy with organizing things, I might have overlooked correspondence.'

'Who cares?' Luca replied irritably. 'They have no right to come here if you don't want them.' He hovered beside her, tapping his fingers on the carved bedhead.

Cecelia pulled her pashmina tighter around her shoulders, as if it offered some protection other than warmth. 'I think we had better let this person make her list. Randolph is so very headstrong and he will cause problems if we refuse. I truly cannot bear any more of his well-meant testiness. It's better not to annoy him and especially now, Luca.'

Luca looked at her steadily, expressionless. 'Well, I'm having nothing to do with it,' he declared, throwing the business card in front of her, stalking to the window and gazing out, arms folded. 'I was looking forward to our special morning but I will go out alone, I have plenty I need to do,' he went on sulkily. 'Don't forget your midday appointment at the salon; you know what you're like when you get distracted.'

Cecelia pressed her hands together, took a breath. 'We'll meet at Le Gavroche at 1.30, then?'

'Yes.'

Cecelia glanced at him, then smiled at me, her engaging social smile which she must have perfected over years at diplomatic receptions.

'Martina, you are such a sensible person as well as a trusted friend; would you be terribly kind and show Mrs Cunningham into the library? She can start her inventory with the scent bottle collection, I have left it there since you so kindly drew me. I will get dressed and be with you as soon as I can.'

I nodded, glancing at Luca. I was puffed up at being

given this significant role but was worried that it might displease him. He followed me from the bedroom, calling my name quietly.

'Little Marti!'

'Yes?' I said, turning.

He stepped towards me and took my wrists lightly, circling them with his fingers. 'Cecelia wishes to keep the peace with her cousin; so be it, but I know that she is terribly upset by this visit. She is too polite for her own good, a lady through and through. I know also that you wish us well, so please, do not engage in conversation with this woman, this interloper. Just show her what she needs to see and let her get on with it.'

'OK. You can rely on me.' I had a sudden urge to stroke the stubble on his chin. I swallowed, my wrists warm within his grasp.

He looked at me. 'You are a gem of a little Marti,' he said, 'a true comrade.'

'Can I have my hands back now?' I asked, emboldened by this praise, attempting flirtation.

He kissed the insides of my wrists and placed my arms by my sides.

'Hands fully returned and in good order. Actually, you have beautiful wrists, very fine bones: an artist's wrists.' He smiled. 'Oh dear, I have made you blush. I am a naughty boy sometimes, I hope you forgive me?' He beat his chest with a closed fist, singing, 'Mea culpa, mea culpa, mea maxima culpa!'

I laughed, delighted and he backed away, hand still on his chest, to Cecelia's room, calling out that he was on his way and the birthday girl had better be up and about!

I drifted to the drawing-room, holding my wrists, giddy with happiness. Mrs Cunningham was examining a decanter on the sideboard and tapping a stiletto-shod foot on the floor. She was a short, plump woman in a tight red suit, with gold hoop earrings and a beaming smile. She carried a briefcase and looked surprised to see me. I explained that Cecelia would be with her soon and led her to the library where she bent to look at the collection with a knowing eye.

'Beeyootiful,' she said emphatically, opening her brief-case and taking out a pen and clipboard. She clicked the pen and wrote the date in large, rounded letters at the top of her lined page. 'Are you a relative of Mrs Buchanan's?' She had a laugh in her voice, as if she found her work hugely amusing.

'No, a friend. It's her birthday today, I'd brought her a card.'

'That's nice,' she said, nodding, starting to write with wide, swift hand movements.

I felt in the way but didn't want to leave because Cecelia had implied that I should stay with her unwelcome visitor. I leaned my forehead against a cool diamond window pane and looked out. The woman opposite, whom Cecelia thought common, was out on her balcony, watering plant tubs and dead-heading petunias. Fortunata appeared from around the corner with two full shopping-bags, placing them on the pavement with a little bobbing motion as she stopped to speak to Elena, who was wheeling out the scooter she used to travel between her cleaning jobs. They both looked up at the window and I waved but they didn't see me, their heads closing together again. Fortunata was gesturing, talking animatedly and it struck me that she spoke so rarely, I couldn't clearly recall what her voice sounded like. Elena shrugged her shoulders, donned her helmet and kick-started her scooter.

Mrs Cunningham had moved to the opposite wall and was writing down the titles of the Fergusson and Cadell paintings hanging there. Her pen flowed smoothly, itemizing; she could have been writing a shopping list.

'I prefer the Cadell,' I told her, suddenly wanting to show off, demonstrate my familiarity with my surroundings. 'He was influenced by Cézanne. They're the Scottish colourist school, you know, they're known for their use of light and colour.'

She chuckled, hitching her skirt up. 'I didn't, but thanks for telling me. I'm just a list-maker, you understand. I like Jack Vettriano myself; he's a Scot, isn't he? But I see enough in my travels to tell that this stuff cost a pretty penny. Those perfume bottles; it's crazy that Mrs Buchanan leaves them lying around, they must be worth a small fortune. And I believe some valuables have gone missing?' She glanced at me, a gleam of interest in her eyes.

After my demonstration of knowledge, I felt out of my depth and recalled Luca's instruction not to get involved. 'I don't know, you'd have to ask her. She enjoys the collection, it gives her pleasure,' I said, turning back to the window. Luca was standing below the balcony opposite, talking to the woman who was leaning over, watering-can balanced on the railing. She reached, broke off a blossom and threw it down to him. He caught it, sniffed it and passed his hand across his forehead. She laughed, shaking some droplets from her can on to his head. He mimed hair-washing, waved to her and strode away.

I felt a sudden anguish, as despairing as I had been thrilled just minutes earlier; the day that had held so much promise seemed to have been tainted. There were long hours to fill before the party; I had intended to ask Luca if I could help with the arrangements, manoeuvre proximity to him, become an indispensable assistant.

Cecelia arrived, dressed but still pale without her make-up. She looked annoyed, her stick tapping sharply on the floor. Mrs Cunningham was impervious to her curtness, treating her with the same joviality, mentioning the glorious weather.

'I realize I'm about as welcome as Ian Paisley in the Vatican,' she said cheerily. 'I'll be as quick as I can, I promise.'

As I left the flat a huge explosion of flowers was being delivered by Connoisseur Cuisine who as always, was running Cecelia's home entertainments. There were arrangements of ferns and ornamental grasses in brass planters. I helped to carry bouquets of apricot and white roses through to the dining-room where two of Connoisseur Cuisine's staff, dressed in green tabards, were setting out vases. A heavy square box filled with silver cutlery lay open on the table where Fortunata was seated, buffing each piece with a dark-blue duster before replacing it carefully in its velvet nest. There was a heady aroma of flower-scents and polish; the smell of the good life. I inhaled deeply and watched as the silver's gleam deepened and blossoms, branches, sprays and leaves were trained into magnificent displays.

*

How excruciating and fantastic it was to be a thirteen-year-old in the tight embrace of infatuation; I started preparing for the party, with its 8 p.m. start, at four o'clock. My hair posed the biggest dilemma; after washing and conditioning it I tried it in a knot, a pleat and a ponytail, but none looked right. I applied mousse, which I disliked and washed out again. Finally I settled on pulling it back with a clip at the base of my neck. My Audrey Hepburn dress had been dry-cleaned and was hanging demurely in its polythene cover. I wiped Cecelia's present once again, ensuring there was no dust on the glass, polishing the frame. I was pleased with it. I wrapped it carefully in a grey metallic wrapping paper with thin silver stripes that had cost me more than the frame and tied a silver ribbon across diagonally. Inspired by Luca and wishing to mimic him and court his attention I had found a quote to write on the gift card;

First you are young; then you are middle-aged; then you are old; then you are wonderful.

My mother rang as I was painting my toenails with a clear, pearly varnish.

'Have you been lonely on your own?' she asked, sounding tired but perkier.

'No, not really. A bit quiet at times, I suppose. Are you better?'

'On the mend and getting back to normal, thank goodness. It's a horrible illness. Your granddad has been an angel in human form; he's taken Ursula and Gregory to the park this afternoon. He'll be back with you on Monday, anyway.'

'Great. His cooking's better than mine.'

'It's the big party tonight, isn't it – Mrs Buchanan's?'

'That's right. Should be good.'

'Well, enjoy yourself. You'll be back with us in a couple of weeks, we'll all be glad to see you. It's been a strange time, all round. I don't like the family being apart, it feels sort of fractured, unreal.'

I stared at my toes. It was the thought of returning that was unreal to me, of going back to the mayhem, back to my mother's all too evident and contagious grief. She seemed miles, continents and oceans away, knowing nothing of the life I was absorbed in. 'I'd better go, you know, got to get ready. Glad you're all healthy again.'

'OK – oh, did you get something nice to wear?'

'Hmm, a dress, just simple.'

'Oh good, I am pleased. Well, take care, I'm doing shepherd's pie for tea so I'd better get chopping. Loads of love from here.'

I banished a quick image of my mother with her apron on, hair bunched back, skilfully wielding the potato-peeler. I had sat with Cecelia while she mulled through the menus provided by Connoisseur Cuisine, finally settling on the one she thought achieved the correct balance without being too formal. That was when I learned that there was such a thing as a fish course. I read her choice with anticipation, memorizing the dishes of this wonderful-sounding feast that I would have to look up:

Parma ham and melon with fruits

*Seared red mullet finger, ginger stir-fried vegetables,
herb butter sauce*

*Roast duck breast, glazed apple fondant, cassis
sauce,
baby roast potatoes with rosemary and puréed
vegetables*

*Summer pudding, Chantilly cream, crushed rasp-
berries
Iced white chocolate and lemon soufflé parcel with
blackberry compote*

I returned to my preparations, applying a second coat of nail varnish and mulled over how I was going to maintain contact with the life at Dauncey, with Luca, when I was back in Watford. My ardour had turned me into a dreamer and schemer, all my energies devoted to sustaining proximity. I had an idea and was planning to discuss it with Bres. I had noticed that there were architectural drawing classes advertised at a college nearby, with a Saturday schedule for the autumn; it included trips to major museums and landmarks. My proposal was that I would attend them, coming to London on a Friday after school; my drawing would benefit from the challenge and the locations. I had the argument all prepared; I knew that my mother would be won over by the idea that I would be developing my talent and I was sure that no equivalent would be available nearer home. Friday evening would be a beacon in my week and I knew that Luca usually stayed in that evening with Cecelia; I was sure that I would become a regular visitor, popping in to say hello after I arrived, invited to dinner regularly.

I wriggled my toes and because I was going to be banqueting while my mother served up mashed spuds, I passed the hours until it was time to dress working on my design for my father's memorial plaque. I had decided on a circle of wild flowers: glory of the snow, agrimony, red campion and Irish lady's tresses – with his name woven through the leaves and stems.

11

Until 11.15 precisely the party was everything I had expected and hoped for. Luca opened the door to me, an auspicious beginning for someone who was by then hooked on signs and portents. He kissed my hand.

'Goodness,' he said, taking a step back, 'I think my eyes need testing! Is this really little Marti or has she sent an older sister in her place? You look amazing. Turn around.' He drew a circle in the air.

I turned, eyes closed, my breath shallow. 'Do you really like my dress?'

'It's perfect, understated.' He stepped closer, whispered in my ear. He smelled of amber and jasmine. 'When you see the horrible floral skirts that are being inflicted on us tonight, you'll appreciate how wonderful you look. Let me just fix your hair a bit better at the back.' He stepped behind me, adjusting my clip, tightening its grasp. One of his cufflinks, his gift from Cecelia, grazed my neck, cool against my flushed skin. I squeezed my hands into fists. 'There, my lovely little Marti. Now, come through.'

Cecelia looked elegant in her gown and simple jewellery.

Her hair had been coloured a deeper brunette and spun into a gossamer halo, secured by a crystal side tiara, shaped like a flower spray. Luca was handsome in a pale-blue linen suit with a white shirt, but then as far as I was concerned, he would have looked striking in a bin bag. The other guests were Wilhelm, Beatrice, Leandra and Ivan Karastov. I saw Luca's point about the other women; Beatrice and Leandra appeared to have bought their skirts at the same shop: gaudy floral patterns, full in line and with bits of lace at the hem. Cecelia and I shared a quiet stylishness; I was over the moon.

Before dinner, we gathered in the drawing-room for champagne dispensed by Connoisseur Cuisine staff and the opening of presents. Luca's was, of course, the first to be unwrapped. Cecelia drew out a plain black box, about a foot long, and took from it a sculpture in beechwood of a man sitting with a lute, one leg crossed over a knee.

'Oh!' she said, holding it with both hands, gazing, then lifting it so that we could all see. 'Luca, how wonderful; it is you, so much you. Thank you, my darling, for such a thoughtful and beautiful gift – the gift of yourself.'

I thought she was about to cry but she shook her head and passed the sculpture to Wilhelm. Luca raised his glass to her, smiling.

'I thought and thought about what I should get you for such a special birthday. And then, it came to me as I was singing to you one day. I had to sit still for some time, Cecelia – not easy for me, as you know!'

She beamed at him, raising her glass in return. Wilhelm passed the sculpture on to Ivan, barely glancing at it. True to form, he was already on his second glass of champagne.

Cecelia continued with her presents: Swiss chocolates from Beatrice and Wilhelm, a blue chiffon scarf from Leandra and from Ivan, a Russian papier mâché box decorated with vivid oranges and browns, telling the story of Prince Ivan and the Firebird. Daphne, who was wearing her own pink satin bow on her collar, picked her way through the discarded paper, sniffing and pawing at trailing ribbons, poking her nose at any glass that had been left carelessly at the side of a chair. Cecelia paused, calling her a naughty pussums, and dipped a finger in her own glass, offering Daphne drops of champagne which she licked eagerly. I waited anxiously while my gift was unwrapped. Cecelia nodded, thoughtful, holding it in her lap.

'This is lovely, Martina,' she said, 'and such a considered and considerate present. Thank you. The quotation, I believe, is Lady Diana Cooper; I met her a couple of times in Nice. If I may say so, you look so pretty tonight, doesn't she, Ivan?'

'Indeed. Promise being fulfilled in more ways than one.'

My cup was overflowing. Unusually, I refused a canapé, my abundant happiness was sustenance enough.

Luca sat at the harpsichord then and played Happy Birthday while we all sang and more champagne and canapés were served. I looked at Cecelia who was pretending to conduct, her slender fingers trembling a little dance in the air. She was smiling but her eyes looked tired, drooping slightly at the corners.

When we went to the dining-room everyone gave a gasp of pleasure; it was as if Connoisseur Cuisine had created a magical stage scene, a scented glade at dusk. The light came from scores of tall white candles casting a golden glow on the foliage and blossoms. The table was decorated with white roses wrapped in leaves and silver-and-white butterflies; garlands of the same butterflies circled the mantelpiece and chandelier. At the centre of the table was a shallow glass bowl with rose heads and floating candles. A little silver fingerbowl of white and apricot rose petals in water was placed by each setting. The cutlery gleamed, the white china and crystal glasses sparkled. Oh Dad, I thought; I hope Heaven, if it exists, has dinner like this laid on for you every evening.

Cecelia and Luca sat at either end of the table; he pulled her chair out for her and made sure she was comfortable before taking his seat. As the starter was being served and wine poured, Cecelia thanked everyone for coming; it had been a perfect day, she said, apart from the intrusion in the morning but one had to rise above such things.

'I shall have words with Randolph when he returns,' she said sparkily, 'he can be sure of that.'

Ivan stopped cutting his melon, waved his fork thoughtfully. 'He is your only family now, madame; families should look after each other. He only means well, he has your interests at heart.'

'Perhaps,' Cecelia conceded, 'but there can be a fine line between interest and meddling.'

Luca nodded. 'You are right, Ivan; families should indeed care for each other, I believe this very strongly too.'

Cecelia cast a puzzled look at him but he had started to talk about a forthcoming concert and how much rehearsing he was doing for it. Wilhelm leaned back in his chair, playing with one of the butterflies; Beatrice was eating quickly, having requested more ham, mopping her plate with bread.

'When do you hope to turn professional?' Leandra asked.

'In the next year or so; my teacher says it is now just a matter of timing and luck. When we return from Tahiti, I am going to seek an agent.'

There was talk then of the holiday planned and holidays past; Cecelia, it seemed, had been nearly everywhere in the world.

'I *am* looking forward to the sun,' she said, 'but home is where I really prefer to be now. Luca has itchy feet though, don't you, dear boy?'

'Yes, but you also need a break, *namrata*; you perhaps don't realize it but the winters treat you harshly. You must soak up some tropical warmth.'

The food was served and eaten, wineglasses replenished – there was a special redcurrant-and-grapefruit cordial for me – and as dusk fell outside, the candle glow grew deeper, the shadows softer. Wilhelm spoke of his plans to travel to Malaysia, Beatrice of her wish to study jewellery design. Leandra asked Ivan if he would make a dress for a wedding she had been invited to and he started to draw designs for her on a little notepad he took from his pocket. Cecelia sat back in her chair; as always she had eaten just mouthfuls of every dish and she managed only a spoonful of her summer pudding. I saw her close her eyes for a moment; when she opened them she looked at me but her gaze was far away, opaque, and I wondered where she had briefly travelled to. Luca said little. I stole glances at him and each time he was smiling, relaxed, eating heartily.

Coffee and liqueurs were served; Wilhelm had such a huge glass for his brandy, I thought he might dive into it.

Once Cecelia had taken sips of her strong black coffee she became invigorated and declared that as was the usual custom, we must all sing now for our supper and 'do a turn'. Beatrice sang 'The Lemon Tree' in a high, coy voice, Wilhelm took a harmonica from his pocket and played a wailing blues number, I reprised my W.B. Yeats, Ivan sang a melancholy song in Russian, Leandra recited *If* by Kipling and Luca rendered a Spanish dance on his guitar. Cecelia looked down the table at Luca when it came to her turn, drawing herself upright in her chair.

'On this night, this lovely special night, it has to be Emily Dickinson,' she said, clasping her hands in her lap. She was silent for a few moments as if summoning energy:

I have no Life but this –
To lead it here –
Nor any Death – but lest
Dispelled from there –
Nor tie to Earths to come –
Nor Action new –
Except through this extent –
The Realm of you –

She continued to gaze at Luca when she finished. We were all motionless, hushed by this direct and open declaration of love. One of the floating candles guttered, the flame dying. I was holding my breath, my lungs squeezing. Luca rose, walked the length of the table and knelt by her side, taking her hands in his.

'My darling Cecelia, *amorin*,' he said. 'Will you please marry me?'

She bowed her head, rested her forehead against his, then sat up, her eyes shining.

'Oh yes,' she said.

Ivan stood, muttered an *excuse me* and left the room. Wilhelm called for a toast, rattling drunkenly among the decanters. Leandra giggled while Beatrice folded and refolded her napkin. I was transfixed, staring at Cecelia and Luca. I knew that I was witnessing something awful and wrong and I knew, too, that I was shortly going to be sick.

I was sick, too, as soon as I reached our bathroom. I rinsed my face, brushed my teeth and leaned my head against the cool tiles. My stomach felt better and I was almost grateful for the purging but there was some other bitter revulsion still lying in my throat.

It was just after midnight. I felt exhausted but unwilling to sleep. I went out into the garden but deliberately walked away from the forget-me-not pond. I wandered about the perimeters, stopping to look at the sky, the dark shapes of bats flittering.

I smelled the cigarette smoke before I heard Beatrice's voice, then Luca's. They seemed to be walking too. I backed behind a broad sycamore, pressed myself against the railing. I couldn't see them, just heard them as they passed slowly, their voices ebbing and flowing like the tide.

'Don't go on, Beatrice, you're boring me,' Luca said.

'I just don't get it; it was all going so well.'

'I know what I'm doing. If you don't like it, clear out. Head off with Wilhelm.'

'You've gone too far this time, I'm telling you. Willi thinks so too. You'll bring trouble now.'

'Oh, sing another song, why don't you? Why do women have to nag so much?'

They faded. A trace of smoke lingered. I held on to the tree, clung for a long while to its sturdy presence.

I fell asleep eventually in the early hours and was woken by the phone ringing. It was nearly half past ten.

'You sound groggy,' Bres said. 'Have you taken to wicked ways with me gone, have you been dancing the night away in the fleshpots?'

'I just woke up,' I said grumpily, my temples throbbing. 'Cecelia's party went on late.' I blurted it out, too distracted and sick to care. 'Luca asked her to marry him.'

'Oooh. Well, I can't say I'm that surprised. And she accepted?'

'Yes.'

'Quite an evening, then, and quite a journey for Mr Gonzi; fisherman to wealthy husband. The cat will be among the pigeons. Did you have a good time?'

'The food was great. It was OK, I suppose.' I shuddered at the memory of it, at my stomach's rejection of it.

'Righto. Well, things are tickety-boo here, or as near as can be. I'll be back about 11 a.m. tomorrow. Get the calf fatted and the cakes baked and the dancing girls dancing.'

'Whatever, OK.'

'I can tell you're the worse for wear so I'll sign off. Your mum will ring later; she's having her hair done, something exotic called a body wave. The twins are watching cartoons and eating raisins. I recommend scrambled eggs and strong tea to lift the spirits. TTFN.'

The idea of eggs was nauseating. I made weak tea and

sipped it accompanied by a slice of dry toast. I chewed slowly, then took two aspirin and went to lie on my bed again until my head stopped aching. My Audrey Hepburn belle-of-the-ball dress was lying on the bedroom floor. I looked down on its crumpled shape; it represented my stupidity, my ridiculous aspirations, my gullibility. I got up, scrunched it roughly and shoved it to the back of the wardrobe. I never wanted to see it again. *He asked her to marry him*, I told myself aloud because part of me was still trying to disbelieve; *he asked her to marry him and she said yes.*

Although the morning was warm I was chilled. I ran a hot bath. I felt estranged from myself, from everyone. I thought of my mother sitting in the hairdresser's with a magazine. She had attempted a perm previously but the stylist had given up in despair when the rollers kept springing out; she had told my mother that her hair was too stubborn. My father laughed when he heard the story, saying it was just like its owner and my mother advised him he would get a clip round the ear if he didn't mind his manners. I knew that that was the true essence, form and texture of love but the knowledge had temporarily escaped me. I lay there for a long time, topping the water up as it cooled. I wouldn't have minded staying there for ever in a warm womb.

Gina came knocking just as I had dressed, asking if I would help her strim the grass by the ponds. She was wearing a wide Australian bush hat with little corks hanging from it.

'I'm dying to know all about last night. I heard there was a proposal. Cecelia went to church this morning looking as if every day was Christmas.'

'How do you know about the proposal?'

'Everyone knows. Sylvie told me; I think she heard from the slimy Wilhelm. I believe Luca actually knelt down?'

'Yes. He knelt down and took her hand and looked into her eyes.' I made myself say it and picture it.

Gina was wielding the strimmer. It made a high, whining sound, like a huge gnat, that put my teeth on edge. She didn't actually need any help; it was a pretext to find out about the events of the birthday dinner. The corks bobbed on her hat as she circled the water-lily pond.

'So, what did Ivan say?'

'Nothing. He left the room just after Cecelia accepted and he didn't come back. He told the Connoisseur Cuisine staff he didn't feel well and to give his apologies. Beatrice wasn't pleased, I heard her tell Luca that he'd gone too far.' I dead-headed a couple of roses, pinching the heads between my fingers. 'You said that about Luca once, that he'd go too far.'

'Did I?' Gina shrugged.

'Yes, we were here in the garden. Is that what you meant, that you thought he would marry Cecelia?'

She switched the strimmer off for a moment, pushed her hat back. 'Not that exactly; even I couldn't have predicted that particular bravado. I've just always reckoned he was a man who'd push as far as he was allowed and then some more. You look a bit pale, are you OK?'

'Just ate too much. Do you think it will really happen, the marriage?'

'If Cecelia has her way, yes – and she does, usually, you know. I think she'll find that she's bitten off more than she can chew, though. Once Luca's got marriage under his belt, he might not be so attentive and indulgent, so full of *amorin* and *namrata*.'

She mimicked Luca so accurately that I winced. She must have noticed because she dug a bag of wine gums from her pocket and offered me one.

'I know you like Luca,' she said, 'and I can see why, he's got a certain appeal, even if it's dubious.'

I held my lime-coloured wine gum up to the light. It was almost the same shade as peridot, Cecelia's birthstone. 'Actually, you're wrong about that,' I said nastily. 'I can't stand him, he's a snake.'

'Oh. Oh, right. I got that arse backwards, then.' She chewed, looking at me, taken aback by my vehemence.

I said I couldn't stay; I had to go and do some cleaning as Bres was due back soon. My father had said that there were few troubles that a bit of energetic hoovering couldn't help. I vacuumed throughout the flat, shoving the machine aggressively before me, thinking about that persuasive voice, that light touch, that particular way of casting a net and making a catch. I was glad when I banged my shin on the edge of the kitchen door, pleased with the vicious pain and the tears it brought to my eyes. I sat on the floor, the vacuum pipe in my hand, the machine still droning. I started to cry, long shuddering gusts of misery. I let the vacuum continue its own melancholy wail so that no one would hear me sobbing for my father.

In the afternoon, I was sitting in the garden when Cecelia came out on to her balcony and called to me.

'Martina, do come up and see me! Luca and the others

are playing tennis and solitary Sunday afternoons can seem so long. I'll leave the door open.' She turned away immediately, accustomed to a quick response.

For the first time since my introduction to Cecelia I approached her flat reluctantly. I had no wish to see her or speak to her. Now I saw her as others perceived her, as a foolish and egotistical old woman rather than my gracious patron. I felt deluded and wrought with a self-loathing at my own stupidity; it seemed to me that she as well as Luca had betrayed me, which was ridiculous and unjust but my victim status allowed no quarter to feet of clay. I trudged slowly up the stairs and loitered on one of the landings, looking out on the treetops. To my jaded eye, the flower-beds and vegetation seemed dusty and faded in the bright afternoon light.

Cecelia was in her bedroom, where she had made room on a shelf for Luca's gift.

'There you are,' she said, 'I thought you'd been kidnapped! I think that's the perfect place for it, don't you? And I am going to have your sketch hung on the wall by the window.'

'It looks great,' I mumbled.

'Wasn't it a wonderful party, a wonderful evening?' She ran her fingers over the carving, over Luca's arms.

'Lovely.'

'I feel like a girl of eighteen again, you know. We are planning to have the wedding at the end of September, so that Tahiti can be our honeymoon trip.'

I looked at her and my distress must have shown on my face because she fiddled with her cuff.

'You seem rather tired, Martina, around the eyes. Are you feeling unwell?'

'I am a bit. I think it was the late night, that's all. I won't stay long, if you don't mind, Cecelia. Bres is coming back tomorrow and I have to get things ready.'

The sun was gleaming on the precious scent bottle collection, illuminating the turquoise of the Palais Royal, sparking a fiery glow on the deep cranberry of an oval Czech atomizer. I moved over to the table, drawn by the beauty of the glass.

'You've moved the collection back here.'

'Yes, darling Beatrice and Leandra brought it through for me last night; I do prefer to have it here so that I can gaze on it first thing in the morning. Martina dear, I understand that you must be fatigued. We did keep you up rather late and the champagne was heady – it doesn't always agree with young constitutions. You know the saying: champagne or high heels – one must be prepared to suffer for them! But before you go, I did want to make one very special request of you: would you be my bridesmaid?'

As I heard the words and felt a nausea rise again in my throat, I saw that there was a space at the back of the collection, where the Thomas Webb fuchsia cameo usually stood. A horrible relief at the avoidance offered lightened my voice. I turned to Cecelia who was smiling expectantly.

'Have you moved one of the bottles?' I asked.

She blinked, her head trembling. 'What?'

'I think that one of your collection is missing, at the back; the Thomas Webb.'

'Are you sure?' She stumbled across to me and held my arm.

'You see?' I pointed. 'It was the Thomas Webb there, wasn't it?'

'Yes, it was. I just . . . I don't understand. There is no reason for it to have been moved.' Her hold on my arm became an uncomfortable pinch. 'Do you think that woman took it, the one who was here yesterday?'

'Mrs Cunningham?'

'Yes.' She passed a hand across her eyes.

'I don't know. It seems unlikely; it would be a bit obvious to steal when you're doing an inventory, wouldn't it? I mean, you would know you'd be a suspect. Maybe when Beatrice and Leandra were carrying the collection back here it fell somewhere? They might not have noticed.' Beatrice was so clumsy, I thought, it was the most likely explanation.

'Fell? Fell? Oh my heavens, what shall I do?' She moved slowly to a chair, her right foot dragging on the carpet a little and sat, staring at the floor.

The doorbell rang, making me jump, followed by several sharp knocks. 'Cecelia, Cissy, are you there?'

I recognized Randolph's voice. 'Shall I get that?' I asked, hoping to dart away as I let him in.

Cecelia was slumped, fingering the pleats of her dress. I moved over to her.

'Shall I answer the door?' I asked again.

She nodded as Randolph boomed her name several times. She looked up then and put a finger to her lips, speaking *sotto voce*: 'What is he doing here? He's not due back until the end of the week! Please, say nothing about the bottle. And stay, please, Martina? Perhaps you could uncork some wine for me; a Barolo is needed, I think. I do feel rather drained, suddenly.'

She looked at me in way that was unexpected, unusual;

with a vulnerable, exposed gaze, as if I was the one in charge. I shrugged. I felt disengagement, both painful and liberating; it wasn't my business to say or not say about the bottle, I thought, as I turned the doorlatch and stood back. Randolph brushed past me, ignoring me, heading into Cecelia's room. He was wearing a white suit, a panama hat and a deep scowl.

'What in God's name have you been up to now, Cissy?' I heard him shout as I opened the kitchen door. I didn't have to eavesdrop as I headed to the wine rack; both their voices were raised.

'Don't yell so, Randolph! What are you doing here?'

'You know full well, you silly, daft, batty old woman! I flew back this morning, as would anyone sane after hearing about your proposal!'

'Who told you?'

'Ivan, of course! He rang me in the early hours. Lucky for you that you have some *true* friends in this world!'

There was much more in this vein as I found a dark-red wine with the Barolo label, uncorked it and placed it on a tray with two glasses. My heart was beating fast as I deliberately loitered, opening cupboards in search of biscuits. Eventually I discovered a tin of Highland shortbread and fanned some of the square slices on a plate, licking sugar dusting from my finger tips. The sugar didn't taste sweet, just gritty. Cecelia's voice climbed the scale, frail but high as they ripped into each other. I sniffed at the tip of the wine bottle, trying to smell the tar and roses the label mentioned. The acrid tar was certainly there; the roses escaped me. My eyes were watering; I hated hearing such anger and discord. I wanted to yell at them to stop. Instead,

I secured the lid on the biscuit tin and replaced it, aligning it carefully on the cupboard shelf.

'I'll put a stop to it somehow!' Randolph was threatening. 'You mark my words, I'll consult the law! There's no way that bastard Luca is going to get his hands on you and your property and money, I'll have you . . . certified, or whatever it takes!'

'Oh, how very Victorian and overbearing of you! Poor Randolph, you're so hopelessly old-fashioned but you must understand.' Cecelia's tone became dangerously saccharine. 'You see, I changed my will recently; Luca inherits almost everything anyway – he doesn't *have* to marry me, he *wants* to. I realize that you find that hard to comprehend, but it's true so you will just have to accept it. I have left you a couple of paintings, by the way, some valuable ones, so you needn't feel too much chagrin.'

'You can't mean that, Cissy! You can't throw away everything you and Olly worked for together!'

'Oh, Randolph, Randolph. Olly's dead and has been for some years. Perhaps you miss him more now than I do. I've "moved on" as I believe the parlance has it these days. Perhaps you should do the same?'

I seized the opportunity of the ensuing silence to take the tray to Cecelia's room. Randolph was staring at the ceiling, his hat in his hand. Cecelia was still in her chair, pallid but with flushed cheekbones.

'Thank you, Martina,' she said, gripping the chair arms tightly. 'And biscuits, too! You are so kind.'

I placed the tray on her table, the one on wheels that slid across her bed when needed. 'I have to go now,' I said. My legs were trembling.

'Of course. Thank you once more. I shall see you later.'
She smiled at me, or rather offered a fleeting, courteous
attempt at a smile before her lips compressed, working
angrily from side to side.

I was conscious of Randolph's stertorous breathing, his
weighty presence. I turned and walked quickly past him,
closing the front door carefully, quietly.

Cecelia was wrong in her final confident assertion to me;
she never saw me again.

Bres had been back for only a quarter of an hour the next
morning when the phone rang and the world tilted on its
axis yet again. He'd had just enough time to compliment
me on my housekeeping and report that my mother, Ursula
and Gregory were back to full health. I was about to tell him
that I wanted to return home, although not my reason; the
lie prepared on my lips was that I missed them and felt it
was time to help my mother out.

'Yes?' Bres said into the receiver, frowning. 'Who?
Speak slowly, now, Fortunata, take a breath, I can't understand.'

As he listened there was a knock on the door and I
opened it to find a panting Gina.

'Is your grandfather back?'

'Yes, he's on the phone.'

'Tell him to come now, straight away. It's Cecelia, she's
had an accident. I've called an ambulance.'

I followed Gina and Bres as they ran to the stairs. At the
top of the first flight my grandfather turned and asked me
to stay at the front of the flats so that I could tell the paramedics where to go as soon as they arrived. I stood on the

front steps. The street was silent, in that mid-morning lull that often occurs, as if the day is taking a breath, marshalling its strength after earlier activity. The brass plate proclaiming *Dauncey Court* was less bright than usual, missing Bres's daily ministrations. I took a tissue from my pocket and rubbed the city dust from it so that some of the gleam started to return. I heard the ambulance siren, watched as it wailed to a halt, gave instructions to the two men and woman who jumped out. I didn't follow them. I continued with my polishing, working my way into the crevices of the lettering.

They brought Cecelia down on a stretcher, a slight figure covered in a red blanket. I caught a glimpse of an oxygen mask but the paramedics' bulky shapes obscured any other view as they deftly slid her in the back of the ambulance. Gina was with them. She squeezed my shoulder as she passed me and got in behind Cecelia. Bres and Forunata came after them, Fortunata weeping and wringing her hands.

'Shush now, shush. They'll do their best for her,' Bres said, 'she's in safe hands.'

'What's happened?' I asked.

Bres shook his head. 'I don't rightly know. She seems to have fallen getting out of that blasted Jacuzzi yoke. Fortunata found her on the floor. Fortunata, where's Luca, do you know? Or any of the others?'

Fortunata shook her head, burying her face in her hands.

'Have you seen any of them this morning?' Bres asked me. He still had the thin stub of a pencil behind his ear, from where he had been studying the racing pages on the train.

'No, no one.'

He sighed. 'Well, this is a fine turn up for the book, a terrible thing. Isn't it well that I was back? I must make sure the police are informed and secure Mrs Buchanan's flat. Martina, will you bring Fortunata down to us and make her a cup of tea. Go on now, Fortunata, you need to calm your-self, all this wailing and gnashing of teeth won't do Mrs B any good, will it?'

Fortunata moaned, face still dipped, but she moved at my side as I led her down to the basement. The top of her head was below my shoulder; I could see the neat parting in her smooth black hair, smell the lemon beeswax polish that she used on Cecelia's furniture.

And that was the start of the endless pots of tea, weep-ing and scenes of disorder that enveloped life at Dauncey Court in the succeeding weeks.

12

My mother wanted me to return home immediately; how odd that this was now exactly what I wished to hear! My grandfather advised that the police said that I should stay put until they'd had a chance to speak to everyone who had seen or spent time with Cecelia in the days before her accident.

'What will the police want to ask me?'

Bres stroked his chin. 'I don't know exactly, pet; how things were with Mrs B, I suppose. The stuff about the proposal, definitely, I would think. They've said not to talk to anyone in the building, by the way, or anyone associated with Mrs B. So keep yourself to yourself for the time being.' He was distracted; the boiler had chosen that very day to break down and there was no hot water.

I gladly kept a low profile, reading, sketching, watching TV. I had no desire to see anyone and especially not Luca, Wilhelm or Beatrice. I pieced together a picture of what had happened by listening to Bres's phone conversations with Righty and with my mother; Fortunata had found Cecelia on the bathroom floor by the Jacuzzi when she let herself in that morning. No one else was in the flat; Luca and Wilhelm had gone out early to the gym and Beatrice was at work. Cecelia was in intensive care; a possible skull fracture was mentioned. I pictured her lying there, no make-up, her hair in disarray, and thought how much she would hate people seeing her like that.

'Why would Cecelia use the Jacuzzi?' I said to Bres over a hasty Welsh rarebit meal that night. 'She has her own ensuite bathroom.'

'No idea; maybe she wanted to try it out as it was new. It had cost her enough.'

Maybe, I thought, she wanted to lie back and gaze at the shimmering stars. 'Do you think she'll be OK?'

'I don't know, I hope so. She's a good age and the shock of such a thing must be terrible, apart from any injury. Put it this way; she may not make a bride. I expect you'd like to see her eventually, if she's all right, if it's allowed?'

That word, *bride*; it made me want to laugh with embarrassment as I recalled my own flights of fancy. I muttered, clattering my cutlery, aware of Bres glancing at me as he put more mustard on his cheese.

'Anyway,' he said, 'it's best not to speculate about any of it. The police will do their work, they can put all the bits of the jigsaw together.'

I couldn't sleep the night before the police wanted to talk to me. Bres had reassured me that Detective Sergeant Egan was a nice enough fellow and there would be a policewoman with him. Bres himself could also be present, if I liked. I said no, I'd be OK; I didn't want him catching me out in a blush or hearing anything he shouldn't if the detective was cunning and made me reveal dark secrets about my Luca hunger. That was what kept me awake; the thought that the police might sniff out my craziness, find amusement in my girlish passions. I wept, wanting my father's counsel, his cool eye and warm embrace. I dozed at last as the dawn chorus started.

Detective Sergeant Egan was Scottish, a slim grey-haired man with a soft voice and patient eyes. PC Meer sat upright beside him with a notepad and a blank face. Her feet were perfectly aligned in her lace-up shoes. We sat in the living-room while Bres went to deal with the boiler repairers. I saw them both noticing my red eyes. My voice was nasal, blocked inside my head.

'I understand,' Detective Sergeant Egan said, 'that you became friendly with Mrs Buchanan after you came to stay here with your grandfather.'

'That's right, she invited me to tea. She liked my draw-ings and asked me to do some for her.'

'So you saw her fairly regularly?'

'Yes. She took me to her dressmaker's and her jeweller's. She bought me this ring, she was very generous.' I had put it on, as a kind of talisman and I held out my hand.

'Very nice,' PC Meer commented.

'It's my birthstone.'

'So you were up in her flat a fair bit?'

'Yes. I did some of the drawings there.'

'Who did you draw, exactly?'

'Cecelia – and Luca.'

'I see.'

'Are you good at drawing?' PC Meer leaned forward,

eyebrows raised.

'I think so. People say I am. Cecelia said she would be my patron for the summer, she was very encouraging.'

'You must be very upset about what has happened to her.'

'I am. It's awful.'

Detective Sergeant Egan put the tips of his fingers together. 'Have you had much to do with Luca Gonzi?'

I shifted on the leather chair. 'He was often there with Cecelia. I drew him at one of the soirées. They were going to get married.'

'So I believe. What did you make of that?'

My voice was retreating inside my head, growing smaller. 'I thought it was a bit funny.'

'Funny?'

'Well, he's a lot younger than her. But she wanted to . . . so. . . .'

'And other people, what did they think?'

'The same, I suppose.'

'You must have heard other people's opinions about their friendship?'

I sipped my orange juice. Detective Sergeant Egan hadn't touched his water and the PC had refused refreshment.

'People didn't think much of it: Gina, the gardener, and my grandfather and Randolph Smythe, her cousin. Oh and Sylvie Leycroft too.'

'They didn't approve?'

'No, not of Luca or his friends.'

The detective asked me then about the night of the party. I explained about the gifts and the dinner, confirmed who had been there. I described the proposal, staring at the notes PC Meer was making on her pad.

'Was there a sense of shock around the table?' she asked.

'A bit, I suppose. Mr Karastov went pale.'

'Mr Smythe tells us that you were on your own with Mrs Buchanan on the next afternoon, the Sunday, when he arrived. Why was that?'

I explained how Cecelia had asked me up for some company, how she was putting Luca's gift on a shelf. 'I hadn't been there long when Randolph arrived, sounding very cross. Cecelia asked me to open some wine. They were shouting at each other.'

'What were they arguing about?' Detective Sergeant Egan glanced at his colleague's notepad.

'The marriage. Randolph was furious, saying he was going to stop it. Cecelia told him he couldn't and that she'd left everything to Luca in her will. I left then, I found it upsetting, listening to them.'

'Did Mrs Buchanan seem ill at all?'

I thought. 'She looked a bit tired, but she did sometimes, especially if she'd missed her medication. When she went to sit down, her foot dragged a bit on the carpet.'

'Do you remember which foot?'

'Her right one. Do you think there was something wrong with her?'

'We don't know yet; she may have had a stroke.'

'Is that bad?'

'It can be; she may not survive.'

'She was looking forward to going on honeymoon, to Tahiti,' I said. 'It was all planned, Beatrice was going to look after the flat.'

PC Meer winced. 'That's unlikely now.'

I thought of Cecelia in her birthday gown, her expectant gaze as Luca knelt beside her and my eyes filled again.

PC Meer leaned towards me. 'This must be hard for you, especially after what happened with your father,' she said gently.

There was a moment's silence while I blew my nose. Tears were running freely; I had no will or power to stop them.

'Of course, Luca Gonzi will probably still go to Tahiti,' Detective Sergeant Egan said suddenly, casually. 'He's indicated to Fortunata that there's no point in wasting a booked and paid-up holiday.'

My tears flowed in earnest then, at that moment when everything turned irredeemably to ashes. Until that point I had entertained some small nugget of belief that Luca might be well-intentioned, misunderstood by all, including me. I had called him a snake but no one truly wants their hero to transform into a villain. I remembered everything I had heard and witnessed and I loathed him as much as I had adored him before. With shame I remembered my fantasies of a future with him, one in which I had neatly dispensed with Cecelia. As I tasted the ashes in my mouth, I heard myself talking through the flood, a bitter flow spilling forth.

'I thought Luca did care for Cecelia, but I don't believe he did, now. I think he stole her paperweight and her scent bottle, or one of the others did – Beatrice or Leandra – and he knew. I saw him carrying a parcel to an auctioneer one day and that was probably something else he'd taken. Cecelia would have done anything for him, she was always giving him money and things: cuff links, a harpsichord, a sound-proofed rehearsal room. His friends just used her and ate all her food, drank her best wines. I bet she paid for meals they had at restaurants. Wilhelm pretended that Beatrice had nowhere to live, but she had been waiting outside; I expect it was all a set-up. Luca was talking to Beatrice in the garden that night after the birthday party and she said he'd gone too far and he laughed. Randolph was right about him and that was why Luca tried to keep him and Cecelia apart. I wouldn't . . . I wouldn't be surprised if he had something to do with her fall. Maybe they had a big argument like they had before – maybe Cecelia changed her mind about something like her will, she could be a bit changeable. There's no reason why she would use the Jacuzzi when she had her own bathroom, is there? He gets everything if she's made a will leaving it to him, doesn't he? If she dies, he can have all the singing lessons and instruments and holidays he wants, have as many night parties as he likes in the garden and he won't have to buy flowers or be back on time or massage her feet or pretend to be interested in Daphne and tapestry work.'

I dug a handful of tissue into my face and rocked in my chair. Neither of them moved for a while. Then I heard someone get up and the sound of water running. I looked up as the detective placed a glass of water in front of me.

'There, have a drink. You've told us a few things, Martina. I can see how upset you are. I think you've been having quite a time of it here. Have a break now. Why don't you do one of those enjoyable things a teenage girl should be doing; go to the pictures or hang out in a shopping arcade. If you don't mind, we'd like to come back tomorrow and talk again.'

I could only nod.

The following morning, Bres woke me with the news that Cecelia had died. He sat on the end of my bed and patted the duvet.

'She never regained consciousness,' he said, 'which in many ways is a blessing.'

'Do they know what caused her death? Will they have to do a post mortem?'

'I think it's called an autopsy. I expect so and it should explain what happened. The police will be back in an hour or so's time, so get up. Are you sure you don't want me to sit in this time, you were very upset yesterday.'

I nodded. My eyes were still sticky from weeping. Bres had nicked himself shaving and had a square of tissue stuck to his chin. He looked so concerned, I parted with some information.

'The police are coming back because I said I thought Luca might have had something to do with Cecelia's accident.'

He put his lips together in a soundless whistle. 'Well, it's what a lot of people might think – but to say it's another thing. What basis do you have for thinking it?'

'I saw and heard things. I don't want to say any more than that. I shouldn't anyway, should I?'

'No, probably best not to.' He rubbed his head. 'This all seems a bit of a mess, pet. I'm sorry you're involved in it, I never dreamed . . . I shouldn't have gone to Watford and left you, that's the truth of it. God knows what your mother will make of it.'

'Don't tell Mum about the police coming back, Bres. She'll only start worrying and fussing. I've got enough on my plate and there's nothing she can do.'

'Well . . . OK, for now, anyway. Let's see what happens after today. I don't like keeping things from your mother, it doesn't seem right.'

I shoved the duvet back, swung my legs to the floor. They felt light and insubstantial. 'Don't you sometimes say that what you don't know can't harm you?'

'True enough. Let's hope they decide that Mrs B died of the fall or a stroke; that will settle any rumours.'

I saw my blotchy eyes and dull, wraithlike face in the mirror, rubbed my cheeks to make myself feel alive. 'Luca will get everything if Cecelia died of natural causes, won't he? The flat, her paintings and collections, her beautiful furniture and china, all her money.'

Bres straightened my duvet, smoothing it with both hands. 'If that's what her will says, yes. But that's better than any proof of foul play, for her and him and everyone else, isn't it? Poor Mr Smythe will certainly rest easier in his bed.'

I said nothing. I envied Bres's innocence.

After the police left I wandered out for a walk, free to leave Dauncey, glad to escape the confines that had previously embraced me. The police had been kind, Detective Sergeant Egan saying how sorry they were that my friend had died. They were slow with their questions; they were particularly interested in the missing items and the day I saw Luca visit the auctioneer. I explained about Randolph's first visit, what he had said about Luca's circus and noticing the missing paperweight. I described seeing Luca visit Newley & Fromhold but not, of course, that I had been following him all day. We went over the valuer's appointment and my spotting that one of the scent bottle collection had gone. They asked if Cecelia had ever seemed forgetful and I said no; she was sometimes tired but she was an intelligent woman, on the ball. At the end of half an hour, Detective Sergeant Egan asked if there was anything else I wanted to tell them. I knew that I must do Cecelia justice; I didn't want them to think of her as a silly old woman, as I had callously thought of her only a couple of days previously.

'Cecelia had been very lonely after her husband died and when she met Luca, life became meaningful again. She was used to company and socializing, you see; she missed it when she became a widow. That's what she told me, and that's how it was. She was a very generous person. And she was romantic.'

'Maybe she loved not wisely but too well,' Detective Sergeant Egan said. 'That's from *Othello*.'

'Shakespeare?' I nodded. 'I don't know it but Cecelia would have, she was very knowledgeable; she knew about all kinds of things, like you shouldn't wear brown shoes in town.'

PC Meer looked at me as if I was raving. Detective Sergeant Egan smiled, saying she had been a lady of the old school, definitely, not many of them like that left. He said that I could go home now, any time I wanted; he didn't think they'd have any more questions for me and he was sure my mother was anxious to have me back under her roof.

'I suppose you're asking everyone questions and they're all giving you different stories,' I fished as he stood to go.

'It is always interesting, hearing various viewpoints.' He nodded. 'Makes our job endlessly fascinating.'

'You know what they say,' PC Meer told me as she slipped her notebook into her top pocket. 'There are only about five basic story lines in the world.'

'No, I didn't know that. What are they?'

'Different cultures have their variations but all the stories contain a chain of events, starting with anticipation, through things going well, then a frustration of some kind and in the end, everything going wrong.'

'Very cheerful,' Detective Sergeant Egan said, 'but it does ring a bell or two. I suppose we wouldn't be in a job if the going wrong bit didn't happen, so it's just as well for us.'

I continued walking slowly towards the river, wondering what was going to happen, what was taking place in Cecelia's flat, whether Wilhelm and Beatrice were still there. I thought of how my story fitted PC Meer's outline, then cheered myself up a little by reckoning that some stories had things going right after that everything going wrong part, but I couldn't think of any at that moment.

I was startled as Beatrice came up swiftly behind me, falling into step with me.

'I thought it was you,' she said. 'Where are you off to?'

'Just walking. I haven't been out for a couple of days.'

'Poor you; you've been busy chatting to the cops, I understand. Here, come and have a drink.'

She grabbed my arm and steered me towards a restaurant with tables outside. I protested feebly, saying I had things to do but her grip became firmer and we were sitting at a table, Beatrice ordering an espresso and orange juice. She'd had her hair done, shaped with a side parting so that it swung in a smooth bob, and with blonde highlights. It made her look older, efficient. She placed a brown sugarlump on her spoon and dipped it into her tiny white cup, sighing as she put the spoon in her mouth.

'It's the simple things in life that are the best,' she said, 'don't you agree?'

I thought of all the rich, expensive food and wine I'd seen her scoff but I nodded. My orange juice tasted odd and there were pips and shreds of peel in it, which made my throat close.

She sat back, swinging a foot. 'So, what have the cops been saying?'

'Just asking me questions.'

'Such as?'

'About Cecelia, mainly,' I lied.

'Oh. Can't have been easy for you?' She was looking at me steadily, unblinking.

'It wasn't too bad.' I drank some of the nasty juice for something to do and looked down into the glass.

'And stuff about Luca, have they been asking about him?'

'Some.'

She leaned forward. 'So, what have you told them?' She was at her most wheedling, her voice very sweet.

I was going home, I thought wearily; what was the point in not saying? 'I told them . . . I told them I thought he might have had something to do with Cecelia's accident. I shouldn't think I'm the only one who says that, either.'

She folded her arms, formed her lips into a silent whistle. 'That wasn't very nice of you. I didn't think you were that type; you know, spiteful, ungrateful.'

It was said lazily but it stung. 'It's what I think,' I said tightly.

'Soooo . . . who are these other people who want to put their tuppenceworth in, give the pot a good stir?'

'Plenty of people have always thought that Luca was using Cecelia.'

'Gosh, you're very knowledgeable all of a sudden; one minute butter wouldn't melt in little Marti's mouth, next she's sticking the knife in. Luca's always been nice to you, too, putting up with you hanging around, fawning over Cecelia, listening to your unwanted opinions, admiring your second-rate doodles; not much of a way to repay him. There was me thinking you really liked him too!'

My brain felt as if it was boiling, as if my head might explode. There was a little smile on her lips; had she guessed my adulation? If so, might she tell the police, name it aloud?

She shrugged. 'Well, who listens to a kid anyway? Wilhelm's always said you're a bit jumped-up and big for your boots. Then again, it can't be easy being a gawky teenager around the grown-ups, the caretaker's grand-daughter, desperate to fit in.'

'Who cares what Wilhelm says?' I thought it sounded pathetic even as I replied. The deep smart of her words was somewhat eased as I noticed the little art nouveau brooch with topaz stones she was wearing to secure the striped cotton scarf at her neck. 'That's Cecelia's brooch, isn't it? She used to wear it with her Balenciaga suit.'

'Did she?' Beatrice ran her finger over it. 'I don't know about that, I never studied her the way you did, all naïve and star-struck. Luca said I could have it, so there you are. What you've said to the cops doesn't matter, you know, Luca wasn't born yesterday and he's covered on all fronts.'

She motioned to the waiter for the bill, taking a twenty-pound note from her purse. Her stubby nails had been transformed into shapely ovals with a pale lacquer but her fingers still fumbled. I thought of a Bres saying: *you can't make a silk purse out of a sow's ear.*

'Do you think Luca loved Cecelia at all?' I asked.

She threw a couple of coins on to the table and stuffed her purse back in her bag. Then she held her hands out wide in a 'who knows' gesture, shoved her chair back and walked away. I watched her taking her short steps, her hair glinting bright in the sun and realized that she had uttered no word of regret about Cecelia's death.

I sat on for a while, replaying what Beatrice had said, wondering if that was how they had all seen me, including Cecelia: the gawky, annoying caretaker's granddaughter. I recalled that it had been Ivan who prompted Cecelia to invite me to her birthday party and yet . . . and yet she had asked me to the flat several times. Surely she wouldn't have sought my company if she had thought me big for my boots? Then again, those invitations had often come when she was alone and probably bored, seeking diversion . . . my head throbbed. Were all the compliments about my drawing just the adults being kind and indulgent to the bereaved kid from the basement? I felt as if the summer weeks might have been a strange, dreamed interlude; one of those heated, anxious dreams where bizarre events occur, nothing makes sense and you wake up with a dry mouth, not knowing who or where you are. I longed to go home, to be in the place where you are accepted and loved no matter how badly you behave.

On the way back to Dauncey I stopped to take a last look at the board outside the Fife and Drum: *If you're thinking of going on the wagon, make sure you keep on going.*

I was catching an early-afternoon train to Watford. It took me only half an hour to pack and I went for a last stroll in the garden, thinking that I might see Gina, but she had already gone, the filled birdbaths evidence of her recent work. I was relieved in a way; now that Beatrice had skewed everything for me, planted the seeds of doubt, I was uncertain that I had been truly accepted by anyone at Dauncey and I wondered if Gina too had thought me a nuisance. I picked a rose, placed it in the spout of a full watering can and left it by the door of her potting-shed, hoping she would understand. I walked to the forget-me-not pond and looked for the toad but he must have had better things to do that day. I sat for a moment on the bench, my mind blank. I heard Cecelia's bedroom windows open behind me and I turned to look. Luca was standing on the balcony, his hands pressed on the railing, looking at me. His gaze was level, unsmiling, unflinching. The sun slid behind a cloud. I got up and hurried to find Bres, to tell him I was ready to head for the station.

I was subdued on my return and thankful that my mother

and the twins were quiet, too. Ursula and Gregory were cautious around me and my mother explained that they probably couldn't understand where I had been. My mother kept glancing at me curiously but other than saying I had grown, she didn't comment. The house seemed small, crowded and flimsy after Dauncey Court. As I was going to bed on my first night back my mother kissed my cheek and said if I wanted to talk any time, she'd be happy to listen. I nodded, thinking how narrow the stairs were. I never spoke to her about the summer's events and she never asked again.

Around the end of September, Bres visited and told me that Cecelia had died of a massive stroke, which had caused the fall and her injuries. The police, he said, had been in and out of the place for some time. Randolph insisted that Luca had stolen from Cecelia before she died and Luca was taken to a police station for questioning once. There wasn't enough evidence and the upshot of it all was that there were no charges against anyone. Wilhelm had vanished, Beatrice was still hanging around and Luca had the flat up for sale.

'Poor Randolph,' I said, 'he must be stunned.'

'Yes, it's all been a shock to him. He talked about contesting the will but I think his lawyer told him there wouldn't be any point and it would just cost him money.' He cleared his throat, loosened his collar a little. 'Luca asked me to ask you if there's anything of Cecelia's you would like to remember her by. He said that you were very special to her.'

My first instinct was to say no; I had the ring she had given me. But then I thought of the topaz brooch on

Beatrice's scarf, her manicure and expensive hairdo and the worms of doubt she had planted in my mind. 'If Cecelia's tapestry is still there, the one she was sewing, I'd like it.' I couldn't bear the idea that Beatrice might work on it, with her ham-fisted stitching and I thought that it might be a way of atoning to Cecelia for being disloyal to her.

It arrived a fortnight later, a large parcel, still in its frame. I recognized Luca's handwriting on the label. There was no note inside, just the neatly packed tapestry with all the silks in a plastic bag. The needle was still in the centre of a lily. I worked on it that autumn and winter, starting by unpicking Beatrice's mess. Apart from going to school, I stayed in, stitching as the twins careered around, ensuring that there were no imperfections. It was a soothing occupation and it helped to calm my turmoil. I liked to think that it was Cecelia's influence, that tranquillity that occasionally overtook me. When I had finished it, my mother made it into a cushion. I have it still, on my sofa, the colours faded now.

I found that I missed Cecelia more than Luca during those winter months. He had temporarily eclipsed her in my eyes but as I selected threads I heard her dry drawl, recalled her sudden bouts of animation and thought of her many kindnesses to me. As the months went by, I felt and hoped that her thoughtfulness had been meant, not manufactured.

In February the following year, just before the first anniversary of my father's death, Bres told me that Cecelia's flat had been sold for over a million and Luca had flown the nest with Beatrice in tow, no one knew where. Bres had also decided to move on; he was going into business with Eppo and Tullamore Joe, running a house-sitting service which he was going to mastermind from a little terraced place he had bought in Battersea.

At my father's memorial service we planted the sturdy ash sapling in the school grounds, my mother and Mr Roberts wielding spades while Bres and I kept the twins under control. I watched as my plaque was attached to the tree and listened as Mr Roberts said that my father was much missed and no one could replace him. The following day I returned on my own. I knocked ice from the tender, twiglike branches and felt as drained and burdened as the sallow winter sky.

PC Meer had been mistaken, I thought; for Luca, the story had ended with everything going right.